Rhyder answered Gina's question shortly. "It's our wedding night, *Mrs.* Owens. Have you forgotten?" Behind the dryness, there was a hint of a jeer. "Your grandfather wanted you to have a proper honeymoon. He arranged this marriage."

"Grandfather wanted to save my reputation. It was for his sake that I agreed to marry you." Despair made Gina's voice bitter. "It doesn't seem fair."

"Nothing in life is fair; a fact you'll discover when you grow up." His words aroused her anger.

"Will you stop referring to me as if I was an infant!" she snapped. "I happen to be your wife!"

But, suddenly, as if her words had brought full awareness, Gina was afraid. She didn't really know anything about this man....

JANET DAILEY AMERICANA

Janet Dailey
Americana

SUMMER
MAHOGANY

Harlequin Books

TORONTO • NEW YORK • LONDON
AMSTERDAM • PARIS • SYDNEY • HAMBURG
STOCKHOLM • ATHENS • TOKYO • MILAN

The state flower depicted on the cover of this book is white pine cone and tassel.

Janet Dailey Americana edition published March 1987
Second printing May 1988
Third printing June 1989
Fourth printing June 1990
Fifth printing August 1991

ISBN 0-373-21919-9

Harlequin Presents edition published April 1979
Second printing May 1982

Original hardcover edition published in 1978
by Mills & Boon Limited

SUMMER MAHOGANY

CHAPTER ONE

GINA STARED in shocked disbelief. It couldn't be Rhyder! Not after all these years. It was impossible. But those were his blue eyes, startling and clear. Did he recognize her? The gold band of her grandmother's wedding ring felt cold, burning like ice around her finger.

Swiftly she turned away before he saw her and knelt in front of the shallow trough of stainless steel, raised by short legs above the firewood. The synthetic material of her scarlet jump suit didn't protect her knees from the gritty sand beneath them, but Gina was oblivious to the discomfort.

Her heart was pounding like a frightened rabbit's. She was hot and cold all at the same time. It was a mistake, an illusion. Her nerves clamored as she desperately tried to deny Rhyder's presence.

But she wasn't wrong. She couldn't make herself look again. The one glimpse of his tall, lithely muscled frame was enough. Not once in nine years had she ever mistaken anyone else for Rhyder, even briefly. There was no reason to pretend she might have done so now.

No, it was Rhyder, with his jet dark hair that

waved crisply when it was ruffled by a sea breeze. Maturity had added to the hardness of his aquiline features, intensified the aloof bearing that bordered on arrogance. He was still deeply tanned by the sun, increasing the startling contrast of his blue eyes with his dark coloring.

Gina closed her eyes, dark lashes fluttering in memory. The years rolled away and she remembered her response to her grandfather's question the first time he had seen Rhyder, wanting to know who the man was that his young granddaughter was staring at.

"He's from away, summer mahogany," she had answered, falling into the idiomatic speech of her native Maine.

People who neither were born nor lived in Maine were never referred to as foreigners or "furriners," nor classified as outsiders. They were generalized as being "from away."

"Summer mahogany" was a category that indicated that Rhyder belonged to the yachting set. It was a descriptive and picturesque term, considering the sun-browned appearance of the boating crowd that descended on Maine in the summer. It separated them from the regular "summer complaints," an affectionate term for tourists who visited the coastal resorts of Maine.

For the impressionable sixteen-year-old girl that Gina had been nine years ago, summer mahogany became more than just a term. Rhyder personified summer mahogany, with his features appearing chiseled in hardwood and browned by the summertime sun. There had been a raw virility about him, a male vitality such as Gina had never encountered before—or since.

Until now. Gina trembled visibly. She wanted to run before another meeting with Rhyder was forced upon her, but she couldn't. Now that she was here, she had to stay. There was no plausible excuse she could make to leave the party.

"I know the breeze is brisk, but you surely can't be cold, Gina," a female voice chided.

Her head jerked toward the sound, her eyes snapping open, darkly turbulent like the churning green depths of the ocean. Quickly Gina masked the emotional upheaval within as she recognized Katherine Trent, Justin's sister.

"I was thinking of winter, I guess," Gina lied.

"It isn't even officially autumn yet. Don't be rushing the seasons." The admonishment was offered laughingly. "Want to give me a hand packing this?" Katherine pulled a large plastic bag toward the shallow trough, three-quarters full of water. "Justin has succeeded in getting detained by the late arrivals. He manages to do that at every clambake."

Gina smiled stiffly, but didn't comment. "I don't mind helping. Part of the fun of a clambake is the preparation."

Her hands were trembling as she reached into the bag containing the seaweed. Fortunately Katherine didn't seem to notice. Seaweed was added to the water in the trough.

"Most people are convinced that the fun is in eating." Katherine closed the plastic bag and turned to remove the burlap top, saturated with water, that covered the large drum filled with live lobsters.

Stacked on top of each other in the metal drum, the lobsters crawled around with difficulty. Their hard shells glistened in a dark green shade against the seaweed scattered among them. Wooden pegs forced their claws apart, eliminating the danger of physical injury as Gina and Katherine lifted the lobsters individually and set them in the trough of seaweed and water.

When the bottom was covered with lobsters, more seaweed was added, followed by another layer of lobster and more seaweed. The barrel drum was emptied and Katherine turned to the clams, already wrapped in cheesecloth sacks.

A few of the clambake guests drifted over to observe the preparations. Their casual interest heightened Gina's tension. The moment was approaching when she would have to face Rhyder. There were nearly thirty guests at the party and she couldn't hope to avoid him indefinitely.

Mentally she tried to brace herself for the meeting. There was always the slim chance he wouldn't recognize her. After all, she had been sixteen the last time he had seen her. Nine years would have altered her appearance more than they had altered his.

True, her hair was still dark, as midnight black as his, but it didn't fall in long silken strands between her shoulders. It was cut short, waving about her ears to add a touch of sophistication to her appearance. Her eyes remained ocean green, outlined by thick lashes, but were no longer trusting and innocent. Her curves were more womanly now, but her figure hadn't changed that much.

Gina sincerely doubted that he had forgotten her, any more than she had succeeded in forgetting him. Bitterly she resented his second intrusion in her life, and she guessed Rhyder would feel the same when he recognized her.

"Gina!"

She stiffened at the sound of her name spoken by Justin Trent. A sixth sense warned her before she turned around that Rhyder was with him. A forced smile curved her mouth as she pivoted stiffly, carefully avoiding any glance at the man walking beside Justin. But she could feel the rake of narrowed blue eyes sweeping chillingly over her frame.

Her fingers closed tightly over the cheesecloth bag of clams as she fought the waves of panic rising inside her. If she had been given a year, she still would not have been prepared for this moment. Her composure was eggshell brittle, threatening to crack at the slightest jar.

"I've been looking for you." Justin slid an arm around the back of her waist. His hand tightened slightly on her hip in a faint caress.

"I've been right here all along." Her husky laughter sounded false as it echoed mockingly in her own ears. She tipped her head back to gaze into Justin's handsome face. "What do you want?"

His brown gaze lingered briefly on her curved

lips, then shifted to the man watching them. "There's someone I want you to meet. Rhyder, this is—"

"There's no need for an introduction." The interruption was smooth and low as Gina was forced to acknowledge Rhyder with a look. The hard blue eyes sent a cold shaft of fear plunging down to her toes. "We are already acquainted, aren't we, Mrs. O—"

"The name is Gaynes," Gina broke in with a rush. "Miss Gina Gaynes." She underlined her single status.

A dark eyebrow flicked upward in sardonic mockery. "My mistake."

"We all make them," she shrugged in an attempt at lightness.

But Gina and Rhyder knew secretly how accurate her response was, even though it was veiled in ambiguity. Electric currents vibrated the air between them. The high voltage was jarring her and Gina needed to end it.

"Who did you think Gina was?" A half smile of curiosity was in Justin's expression.

An aloof mask was drawn over the tanned features. "It doesn't matter." Rhyder let his gaze swing blandly to Justin. "I think you were going to offer me a drink, weren't you, before we were sidetracked by Miss Gaynes."

"Sure," Justin nodded, removing his arm from around Gina, pocketing his curiosity for the time being. "What will you have, Rhyder?"

"A beer."

"Wait here. I'll get it," he told him and moved toward the opposite side of the crowd.

Gina stood uncertainly for a moment in front of Rhyder, her fingers clenching and unclenching the bag of clams. His alert gaze picked up the nervous movement and she immediately stilled the betraying motion.

"Excuse me," she murmured stiffly, then turned away, taking the few steps necessary to carry the clams to the molding trough.

Rhyder followed leisurely. Gina tried to pretend he wasn't there as she again began to help Katherine, but she was disturbingly conscious of him. He stood apart, watching the preparations with absent interest.

There was little color in her cheeks as she spread another layer of seaweed over the clams while Katherine went after the sweet corn. When she returned with an armload of foil-wrapped ears, Gina took them from her and began woodenly distributing them atop the seaweed-covered clams. Katherine disappeared again for more corn.

An ear of corn rolled to the ground. Gina moved to retrieve it, but it was Rhyder's sun-browned hand that reached it first as he bent beside her. He didn't immediately offer it to her, forcing her to extend a hand, her gaze averted from his chiseled features.

"I wasn't aware you'd changed your name." Rhyder placed the ear of corn in her outstretched palm, speaking low and cynically for her hearing alone.

"I wasn't aware that it was any of your business," Gina retorted bitterly.

The creases around his mouth hardened. His cutting gaze slashed to the gold ring on her left hand. "What about that?" he challenged coldly.

"This?" She lifted her hand, letting the precious metal flash in the sunlight. "The truth is it's my grandmother's wedding ring, the only thing I have that was hers. I have to wear it on my left hand because it's a little too small for my right."

She straightened, feeling a glow of malicious satisfaction at his inability to dispute the truth. Before she could replace the ear of corn, his hand closed over the crook of her elbow. Anger smoldered in his gaze.

The harsh grip dug into her skin, but Gina didn't try to pull away. Her eyes were as cold and green as the winter sea when she lifted her contemptuous gaze to his.

"Let go of me." The order was issued in a demanding undertone. "Or would you rather I called for help?" They were brave words considering the hammering of her heart at the way he towered beside her.

But her words had the desired effect as Rhyder abruptly released her, his mouth twisting in a vicious, jeering line. "You still can't come up with anything more original after all these years, can you?"

Inwardly Gina flinched, but she turned away before Rhyder could see that his sarcastic gibe had hit its target. Justin and his sister arrived almost simultaneously.

There was someone else Justin wanted Rhyder to meet. After handing him the cold beer he had requested, Justin led Rhyder away, pausing to suggest that Gina accompany them. She refused, insisting she wanted to help Katherine.

Katherine was too preoccupied with the arranging of the sweet corn, potatoes, onions, sausage and hot dogs to notice Gina's unnatural silence as she assisted. For Gina, it was a relief when the moistened burlap bags were tucked around the heaping mound of food and canvas covered the burlap. She didn't stay for the lighting of the fire beneath the shallow trough, hurrying to the beachside house with the excuse of washing her hands.

Almost the very instant she stepped inside the quiet house, reaction set in. Her legs trembled so badly she could hardly stand. She collapsed in the nearest chair, feeling nauseated, pain screaming in her temples. Her mind reeled as she tried to take in the implications of this second meeting.

Rhyder had been invited to the clambake by Justin. The two men were obviously on a first-name basis. Rationally, Gina knew the two facts did not mean the men were friends. Justin's gatherings were generally business and pleasure.

Since she could not recall Justin's ever mentioning Rhyder's name in the past—and that was certainly something that wouldn't have escaped her notice—it was possible that Justin was only now attempting to cultivate Rhyder's friendship for business purposes.

It seemed a logical explanation. And it would also provide a reason for Rhyder to be in Maine in September instead of summer. There was no comfort in that knowledge. Gina didn't want him involved even in the remotest sense with her life. She ran a shaky hand across her damp forehead and down a cool cheek. Her concern at the moment was in how long he would be staying.

The irony of the thought twisted her lips in humorless amusement. Nine years ago she had been concerned about the same thing for an entirely different reason. Nine years ago she had dreaded the day he would leave. Now it couldn't be soon enough.

Where was her sense of humor, Gina wondered. She should laugh at the situation instead of being unnerved by it. The nine-year-old episode should be part of the past, an experience to be filed away as part of growing up.

Summer mahogany. He had seemed like a god to her. The sea wind and sun had chiseled the masculine planes of his face in smooth and powerful lines. If Gina had been given to romantic flights of fantasy, she might have regarded him as a knight in shining armor. Perhaps in her subconscious, he had been.

At the time, Rhyder had simply been the most compelling man she had ever met, virtually the first man she had ever been aware of in a physical sense. His latent virility had awakened her femininity as none of the attention from boys in her age group had done. Rhyder had been twenty-six that summer nine years ago. His life-style alone set him apart from everyone else.

Within a few days after seeing him for the first time, Gina had begun subtly trying to attract his attention. Sometimes she was conscious of what she was doing, but mostly she was guided by instinct. Fate and a misbehaving engine in his sleek sailing yacht had put him into the port where her grandfather trapped lobsters. Gina had dozens of ready-made excuses for being around at any hour of the day.

From being a nodding acquaintance, she graduated into passing the time of day and on to chatting briefly. At sixteen, Gina was attractive and unconsciously alluring. The combination of long black hair and green eyes was eye-catching to any male. Rhyder wasn't an exception.

Gina had often seen his veiled gaze running over her face and figure in silent admiration. But he was also aware of her youth and the nearly ten-year difference in their ages.

She remembered the afternoon she had gone to the beach for a swim, with the full knowledge beforehand that Rhyder was there. In her effort to establish a more personal relationship, she discovered a streak of guile within herself that she hadn't known existed.

It enabled her to feign surprise when she saw him in the water, send him a friendly wave, and swim alone as if she didn't mind sharing the secluded cove with him. Later, when she had waded ashore, he was sunning himself on the sand, his muscled chest and legs already tanned a mahogany brown.

The sandy beach area of the cove was small, so it was perfectly natural that she had to sit within a few yards of him to dry herself off. His gaze had flicked to her briefly, faint amusement in the blue depths, as she toweled the excess water from her skin.

"It's a beautiful summer day, isn't it?" she had declared artlessly.

"Mmm," had been his sound of agreement, closing his eyes.

For a while Gina had said nothing, hoping to indicate a companionable silence. Then she asked with false idleness, "Have you repaired your motor yet?"

"I'll find out tomorrow," Rhyder had answered. "We're taking it out for a test run."

"We?" Gina had repeated blankly, then nodded understanding. "You're referring to Pete."

She hadn't figured out just exactly what relationship the man was to Rhyder. At times she thought he might be an employee, a deckhand or something. Other times they seemed like the best of friends.

Yet Pete didn't strike Gina as the outdoor sailing type, so if he was a friend, she couldn't imagine him volunteering to have a sailing vacation. He was more at home with books than he was with anything to do with the yacht.

Rhyder was lying on his back, arms raised to rest his head on his hands. He shifted slightly to allow his alert gaze to sweep over her, taking in the jutting firmness of her breasts beneath the one-piece bathing suit of canary yellow.

"How old are you, Gina?" One corner of his mouth lifted in a gesture of mocking amusement.

"Seventeen. I'll be eighteen in August," she had lied, advancing her age by a year.

The lines around his mouth had deepened. "Sometimes you barely look sixteen."

"'Sweet sixteen and never been kissed?'" Gina had laughed throatily. "That's hardly true."

"You look amazingly untouched by all your experiences," Rhyder had replied with deliberate mockery.

Gina's heart had beat faster. She knew Rhyder was beyond her experience. There was an exhilarating sensation of danger in the way she was flirting with him.

"I never said anyone had taken me into the bushes." She had met his gaze levelly, her eyes as clear and as bright as the unplummeted, green ocean depths. "I was only talking about kissing," she had retorted, implying that he had referred to more worldly things of which he knew a great deal more than she did firsthand.

"You've done a lot of kissing?" He had made it a question, a dancing light moving over his face.

Gina had leaned back on her hands, a smug half smile curving her mouth as she lifted her face to the sun. "Oh, once or twice at least."

"Are you good at it?" There was suggestion of amusement in his low voice.

"I'm learning." She had darted him a laughing glance, fielding his teasing questions with lighthearted abandon.

She was enjoying this conversation with its stimulating undertones. She had never traded words like this before, not about making love. It made her feel daring and gloriously wicked.

"Why don't you come over here and show me what you've learned?" Rhyder hadn't shifted from his position—flat on his back, hands under his head, only the blue of his gaze turned to her.

Gina's breath had caught in her throat at the suggestion. There was nothing in the world she wanted more than to find out what it would be like to have Rhyder kiss her. Luckily, before she submitted to his invitation, she had realized that he was only making fun of her. It had hurt, but not as much as it might have if she had childishly taken him seriously.

She had laughed, a forced sound, not quite natural, but she didn't think he had noticed. "No, thank you, Rhyder."

She had rolled gracefully to her feet, holding an end of the beach towel in her hand and letting part of it trail in the sand. She had shaken her head and smiled, her refusal very adult.

"What's the matter? Are you afraid?" The taunt had been gentle and not really argumentative.

"I'm wary." There had been a great deal of truth in that statement. "That's how I've managed to stay out of the bushes." Her hand had flicked blue black hair away from her cheek. "I'd better be getting back so I can start supper for gramps."

To get to the path leading from the beach, Gina had to walk past Rhyder. He had levered himself onto one elbow at her last remark. As she had walked past him, his hand had reached out and caught the trailing end of the towel. He had made a pretense of using it to pull himself to his feet. Once upright, though, he hadn't released the towel.

Something elemental had seemed to hover in the air, charging it with an unknown tension. Absently, Gina had been aware of the pulse beating wildly along her neck, but she hadn't been able to move.

The laughing glint had left his blue eyes as they darkened with purpose. The strong angles of his face had hardened slightly. His grip had tightened on the towel, pulling her toward him. Gina hadn't resisted, drawn by a magnetic force that somehow emanated from him.

With one hand, Rhyder had kept a hold on the towel while his other hand had settled on the naked curve of her shoulder and arm. Liquid fire had splashed from his touch, golden heat flowing through her veins. As his dark head bent toward hers, she had closed her eyes, butterflies fluttering in her stomach.

At the touch of his mouth, her lips had quivered. In seconds, the exploring expertise of his kiss had coaxed a pliant response from her. He had aroused sensations that boys in her age group had not been able to with their awkward and sometimes demanding kisses.

Again instinct had taken over, letting her return the kiss with an ability not gained from experience. Her hand had rested on the bare hardness of his trim waist, more for support from the heady sensations erupting within than from a desire to actually caress him.

When Rhyder had lifted his head, she had been dazed. Her equilibrium had been slow to return under the methodical study of his inscrutable gaze. There had been a faint grimness about his hard features, browned by the sun into vital masculinity.

"I can't make up my mind about you," Rhyder had muttered beneath his breath, seemingly unaware that he had spoken aloud. Almost immediately there had been a crooked lift of his mouth, a mask of mockery covering his expression. "You'd better run along home, woman-child, and fix that supper for your grandfather."

He had given her a playful push in the direction of the path and Gina hadn't minded letting it end there. She had wanted to savor the sensations, remember every one in detail. Rhyder had kissed her and it had been wonderful.

Gina moaned softly at the memory. Why hadn't it ended there with just a romantic dream? If Rhyder had left the following day when his engine had tested out, she wouldn't be going through all this anguish at seeing him again. He would have been just some dark stranger who had captured a young girl's heart and faded into unreality.

But it hadn't happened that way.

The trepidation she had felt nine years ago walking down to the harbor the next day came flooding back. It increased when Gina saw Rhyder's sailing yacht, the *Sea Witch II*, coming in to dock. The engines weren't missing a stroke and she had known the repairs had been successful. There wasn't any reason for Rhyder to remain in this uneventful port.

Since it could have been the last time she would see him, Gina had stood at the dockside, fighting the lump in her throat as Pete clambered awkwardly from the deck to the dock to make the lines fast. Gina would rather it had been Rhyder.

"Everything sounded smooth when you came in," she had commented to Pete after he had self-consciously returned her smile. "You must have corrected the problem."

"Rhyder says so," he had agreed.

"I guess that means you'll be heading out tomorrow." She had hated saying the words.

"No, we're going to stay here and explore the Washington County area. It's too crowded farther along the coast," he had concluded, and it had sounded as if he were mouthing Rhyder's sentiments rather than his own.

But joy had leaped into Gina's heart. If they were staying in the area, that meant she had a good chance of seeing him again.

"There are a lot of dogfish there," she had agreed, hardly able to contain her excitement.

"Dogfish?" Pete had stared at her blankly.

"Summer complaints."

"Summer complaints?" Her explanation hadn't helped him at all.

"You know—tourists," Gina had explained with a wide smile.

"You call tourists 'summer complaints?'" He, too, had smiled broadly.

"We don't mean anything bad by it. Actually it's big business along the coast," she had assured him.

"'Dogfish' is a term for a tourist, too?" Pete shook his head. "But that's a kind of shark. Hardly complimentary."

"But it isn't meant that way," Gina had protested with a laugh. "Handliners—fishermen—almost hate the dogfish because when the haddock should be taken, along comes the dogfish. Tourists start arriving at almost the same time. There are several terms that are used for seasonal visitors."

But Gina didn't mention "summer mahogany." That was special, reserved for Rhyder.

"Incredible!" Pete had breathed, wiping the perspiration from his brow and flipping back a wayward lock of sandy hair.

"Are you getting a lesson in Maine-iac expressions, Pete?"

With a startled, quarter-turn spin, Gina had faced Rhyder. Her heart had skipped a beat at the sight of him, his ebony hair ruffled and tangled by the salty ocean breeze. A cream-colored knit shirt had loosely molded his broad shoulders and leanly muscled chest.

Agilely he had swung from the glistening deck. His blue gaze had skimmed over her, making her aware of the way she was staring. She had looked quickly away as Pete replied, "I certainly am."

A crony of her grandfather's had walked by at that moment, his alert gaze sweeping the trio before he nodded to Gina. "How's Nate?" he inquired, referring to her grandfather.

"Nicely, thank you." She slipped her fingers into the slanted pockets of her jeans. "They crawlin' good?"

"Daow!" he had answered emphatically.

"Gramps changed water in his traps today, too," Gina had agreed as the man continued on his way.

"Would you mind translating that conversation?" Pete had frowned bewilderedly.

A sideways glance had caught Rhyder's amused and interested look. Gina obligingly launched into an explanation of what had been said, aware that she was the sole object of Rhyder's attention and determined to acquit herself intelligently.

"Clyde Simms asked how my grandfather was and I told him he was doing nicely as opposed to poorly—or in poor health. Then I asked him if the lobster were crawling—or moving along the ocean floor and with luck into the lobster traps. His reply was 'daow'—a negative just about as definite as you can get." Gina had smiled broadly. "He would have told you that whether it was true or not."

"What did you mean about changing water in the traps?" Pete had persisted, a curious half smile beginning to curve his thin mouth.

"When a lobsterman goes out to haul and comes up with empty traps that he has to rebait and reset, it's called changing water in the pots. In other words, an unproductive task, since he didn't catch anything."

"I don't think I've ever heard such picturesque speech patterns," Pete had declared, addressing the comment to Rhyder.

"Mostly they come from nautical terms or from the logging days," Gina had acknowledged.

"Yes, but they're still in use. Of course, Maine is pretty isolated up here in the corner all by itself, practically," he had conceded. Rhyder didn't attempt to contribute to the conversation, but stood to one side, listening and watching Gina.

"It may seem as if we're isolated, but it's far from the truth. Look at all the seasonal visitors we get from all parts of the country and the world," Gina had argued. "And Mainers have always been known for their association with the sea, whether it was fishing commercially or shipping. The history of the people is very cosmopolitan. The old idioms linger because they indicate an individuality. "Also—" a bright twinkle had entered her eyes "—it makes us remembered. People come from away, hear the way we talk, and go back to tell all their friends what quaint things we said. Everyone knows word of mouth is the best advertisement. What better way to encourage more tourists to come to our resorts?"

Rhyder had laughed, joined almost immediately by Pete, then Gina. It had been a magic moment, knowing she had made him laugh with her and not at her.

"Brilliantly spoken." Rhyder had smiled at her. "Surely you didn't think I was an empty-headed creature, did you?" Gina had tipped her head provocatively to one side.

"No, I didn't think that." But he had seemed to withdraw, his smile becoming indulgent instead of sharing amusement.

"Well—" she had gazed off into the distance, resenting his sudden aloofness "—I'll be going. See you around." She removed a hand from her pocket to flick a goodbye salute to the two men.

When she had moved away, Gina had felt Rhyder watching her leave. There was satisfaction in that, and in the knowledge that Rhyder wasn't leaving the area, either. She would see him again, soon. Maybe things would work out better the next time. . . .

After all, he had kissed her once. She had lifted a finger to her lips in memory of the thrilling sensation. He would hardly be reluctant to kiss her again if the opportunity presented itself. Gina had hoped that there would be an opportunity, or that she would be able to create one. Yes, she would see him again, soon.

CHAPTER TWO

GINA BURIED HER FACE in her hands, but the haunting memories of the summer nine years ago wouldn't stop. Any moment now she would be missed from the clambake and someone would come looking for her. Rhyder would guess immediately that he was the reason she was hiding.

She wasn't hiding exactly, but that was what he would think. She would rejoin the others, she promised herself, in a minute. Only a minute more in the peace and quiet of the house.

Only there wasn't any peace and quiet, not in her mind. It was noisy with thoughts, especially of another day nine summers ago when she had not found peace along a serene beach.

Gina had poked a toe at the regular row of seaweed, the high-water mark of the tide. She hadn't seen Rhyder for three days, not since the day the engine had been tested. A short piece of driftwood rested above the seaweed, smoothed and whitened by the salt water and sun. Burnished gold grass grew in a sturdy clumps, accented by the lavender purple blossom of the beach pea.

But Gina hadn't noticed these, nor the pale pink of the bindweed flower, nor the colorful shells tangled in the seaweed. Rhyder had left and hadn't come back. Foolishly she had believed that because Pete had said they would be staying in the area, it meant they would be using her small port as a base.

"See you around," she had said confidently, never believing that she had actually been saying goodbye to him.

With a dispirited sigh she had turned away from the beach, toward the headland cliffs and the jumble of rocks, some smooth and some jagged, but all spectacular. Gulls screeched overhead, swooping and gliding in graceful acrobatic acts. Tenacious blue flowers grew out of the rocky cliffs, supple stems bending with the wind.

Although Gina was planning to go home, she took a roundabout route by the harbor, unwilling to admit that Rhyder would never return. She didn't really expect to see the yacht, *Sea Witch II*. She was so certain she wouldn't see it that she nearly didn't. When she recognized it, she took two racing steps toward it before she could control her exultation and saunter casually forward.

Rhyder was on deck, the white of a sail spread across his lap. Gina could see he was stitching a tear in the canvas. She paused on the dock where the boat was made fast.

"Do you sew a fine seam?" she asked mockingly.

He glanced up at her briefly. "Hi, Gina. Come aboard." He bent his dark head again to his task.

She wished his welcome could have been a bit

more enthusiastic and his invitation less like inviting a child aboard. But she was much too glad to see him again to let herself worry about that for long. She stepped aboard with alacrity.

"Where's Pete?" Gina glanced around.

"Ashore buying some groceries so we can eat dinner tonight."

It was on the tip of her tongue to invite them to eat with her and her grandfather, but she sensed that would be going too far, too soon. She leaned a shoulder against a mast and watched him work.

"I was beginning to think you wouldn't be coming back here," she said at last.

He looked up, a mischievous light dancing in his blue eyes. "Did you really think I wouldn't come back to see my girl one last time?"

His roguish glance slid over the golden length of bare legs, then darted up to her face to leave her in little doubt that he was referring to her as his girl. She knew he was only joking, too.

"Come on, Rhyder," she laughed, but tightly. "You're the kind that has a girl in every port."

The insanity of jealousy churned her stomach as she suddenly imagined all the girls he probably had held in his arms. She was only sixteen. What chance did she have of attracting a man like him?

"Jealous?" His eyes crinkled at the corners, but his mouth didn't curve into a smile as he teased her.

"No." Gina straightened away from the mast and tossed her head in proud defiance of the truth. "How could I be? I'm not even your girl. One kiss doesn't make you belong to someone, at least not in the crowd I run around with."

"I keep forgetting how experienced you are." The mockery was low in his voice. "If you want to make yourself useful, why don't you go below and fix some coffee? There's some instant on the shelf by the stove. Do you think you could manage that?"

"I think so," Gina declared, briefly hating him for the way he taunted her. "I've had to become very domesticated since my grandmother died."

The crystal brown of instant coffee covered the bottom of the mugs sitting on the galley counter in front of her. The water was heating in a pan on the stove, bubbles clinging to the bottom and sides. She shifted impatiently, then turned with a start as Rhyder entered the small galley.

"It's almost ready," she said quickly, turning back to the stove.

"No hurry." He slid onto a bench seat behind her. "What happened to your parents, Gina?"

"They were lost at sea when I was only two," she replied unemotionally. She had never really known them, so it didn't bother her to talk about them.

"Was your father a lobsterman like your grandfather?"

"No, he was an attorney, specializing in maritime law, but gramps said he loved the sea. My mother did, too, I guess. They went out whenever they could. One time they got caught in a storm and never came back," she explained.

"So your grandparents raised you," Rhyder concluded.

"They've been wonderful to me." Her voice carried the warmth of deep affection. "Of course, we lost grandma two years ago. The doctors said her heart just stopped. Gramps and I have been on our own ever since. He's a dear."

The water was nearly boiling. Gina lifted the pan from the flames and deftly filled the cups. She set down the pan at the back of the range, turned off the burner, then handed a mug to Rhyder. She started to offer him the sugar and canned milk she had set out, but he waved them away.

"I take it straight," he told her, and motioned her toward the bench seat opposite him. "What have you been doing these last three days?"

"Nothing special," Gina shrugged. *Except waiting for you to come back,* she added silently.

"No heavy dates?" He was mocking her again.

"None." She sipped at her coffee, knowing it was too hot, and nearly burned her tongue.

His gaze ran over her face, blue and glinting. "A young girl as attractive as you are must have a boyfriend or two somewhere around."

Sensitive about her sixteen years, Gina tried not to let it show that it irritated her when he mentioned her youthfulness. And he didn't care whether she had any boyfriends or not. Rhyder was teasing again.

"There are one or two," she agreed with forced calm. There probably were, but Rhyder was the only male who interested her. "But no one special." There was a flash of green fire in the look she gave him, but she veiled it quickly with her black, curling lashes. "How about you?"

"You must have forgotten," he mocked her. "I'm supposed to have a girl in every port. You said so yourself. So how could I have a special one with so many to choose from?"

"That might have been a slight exaggeration," Gina conceded. "But I'll bet you've known a lot of girls. I'm sure there are a lot of girls who are crazy about you." And she hated every unknown one of them with the violent emotion of youth.

"There might be a couple." His tongue was very definitely in cheek; he was amused by her answer and probably guessing that she was one of the girls who was crazy about him.

Gina lifted her chin, thrusting it slightly forward, determined to be adult and womanly. "Do you make love to them? The girls you take out?"

The mockery left the clear blue of his eyes as a dark brow arched at her prying question. "Do you mean, do I kiss them or—how did you put it the other day—do I take them into the bushes?"

The subtle inflection of eroticism in his voice brought a pink glow to her cheeks. Gina bent over her coffee mug, hoping he would blame her rising color on the heat from the coffee.

"I guess I wondered if you were the kind that thought a girl owed you something just because you asked her out," Gina hedged.

"There isn't any such thing as an unwilling

participant in a seduction scene, Gina." Without pausing Rhyder demanded, "Exactly where is this conversation leading?"

"Nowhere in particular." The forbidding line of his mouth made her more uncomfortable. "We're just talking, that's all."

"That's all?" He muttered her last phrase in sarcastic disbelief. There was checked anger in the way he pushed himself from the bench and poured the coffee from his mug down the drain. "Someone should tell your grandfather how dangerous it is to let you run loose. He should keep you under lock and key. You're not even dry behind the ears yet."

"How would you know?" Gina challenged, her eyes smarting with tears at the way he had verbally slapped her as if she were a precocious child.

Hurt drew her to her feet, and she dumped her own coffee into the sink. When she would have turned away, Rhyder grabbed her by the wrist and pulled her around.

"You're hurting me," she protested tightly.

"Someone should teach you a lesson," he growled, and pulled her against him.

His mouth closed punishingly over hers as his arms crushed her against his muscular length. But the pliant softness of her almost womanly curves molding against the hard contours of his body seemed to immediately drain the savage anger from his kiss.

The mobile pressure of his mouth became sensual and arousing. Gina wound her arms around his neck, surrendering with innocent abandon to his assault.

Abruptly Rhyder tore his lips away from hers, and she pressed closer to him, trying to force his head down. "Rhyder, please," she invited.

His jaw worked convulsively as he roughly pulled her arms from around his neck. "You aren't going to play any grown-up games with me!" he snapped. "Go home, kid, and wait until you grow up before playing with fire!"

His eyes were as cold as the winter sky, freezing her with their iciness. With a sobbing gasp, she wrenched her wrists free of his hold and raced past him up the steps to the deck, nearly knocking a returning Pete down in the process.

Once ashore, she checked her blind flight, slowing her steps to a stiff walk. Her emotions alternated between hate and hurt at the way Rhyder had robbed her of her pride. The humiliation she felt was magnified by her young years until she wished the world would come to an end.

For two days she avoided the harbor as fiercely as she had once sought it. The harbor and any place where she might run into Rhyder. Considering the small area of the community, it meant Gina practically had to restrict herself to the house.

The third day her grandfather mentioned that the *Sea Witch II* wasn't at its moorings when he had gone out to haul. And Gina felt free to wander to some of her childhood haunts without encountering Rhyder.

After washing up the noon dinner dishes, she

slipped out of the house. Her grandfather was busy repairing some damaged lobster pots and probably wouldn't miss her until nearly supper. She walked, her pace fast as if she were trying to race to escape the dogging pain. By three o'clock the summer sun and her exertions had made her hot and sticky. The prospect of an ocean swim became decidedly inviting.

She made a brief stop at home to change into her swimsuit and grab a towel, then set out for the small beach where she always swam. She was picking her way along the rocky path down the headland when a movement near the beach caught her eye. She stopped to look, then became paralyzed as she recognized Pete wading ashore. Anguish clouded her eyes as her searching gaze found Rhyder swimming toward the shallow water.

Common sense told her to run before she was seen, but pride insisted that she had to show Rhyder that he meant nothing to her. Childishly she didn't want him to know how severely he had hurt her with his rejection of her love. With a determined toss of her raven hair, she continued along the rocky path to the beach.

"Man, that beer is really going to taste good when we get back to the boat," Pete declared, a breathlessness in his voice from swimming.

Rhyder didn't respond to the comment, and Gina glanced up as she took her first step onto the sand. He was staring at her, grim-faced, and she immediately looked away with a haughty lift of her nose. Pete turned to see what had captured

Rhyder's attention and brought such a forbidding expression to his darkly tanned features.

"Hello, Gina," Pete offered quickly.

"Hi, Pete," she replied, but she deliberately avoided greeting Rhyder and he did the same. Out of the corner of her eye, she saw Pete glancing from one to the other and knew he felt the crackling tension in the air. She dropped her towel on the sand and started slipping off her sandals. "How's the water?"

"Fine," Pete answered uneasily. "Look, er, we were just leaving. If I stay in the sun much longer, I'll turn into a boiled lobster." He laughed uncomfortably, trying to make a joke of it.

In truth, Pete's fair skin was more inclined to freckle than tan, but she knew he was only trying to cover up Rhyder's pointed silence.

"I couldn't care less whether you leave or not," she shrugged, and pushed her sandals under her beach towel.

"Are you meeting someone?" Rhyder suddenly demanded in a curt tone.

Her head jerked toward him, her expression cool and disdainful. "I don't see that it's any of your business, but no, I'm not."

"You shouldn't swim alone."

"I've done it hundreds of times and nothing has happened to me yet. I'm a very strong swimmer," Gina declared.

"Ability has nothing to do with it," he growled roughly.

"Really?" she answered mockingly. "Well, for

your information, I'm also wise enough never to get out of my depth."

"Are you?" His steel-blue eyes touched her mouth and the rounded swell of her breasts in a suggestive look that sent the blood rushing to her cheeks. "You could very easily get into trouble."

"I certainly wouldn't call to you for help if I did," Gina muttered bitterly. "Go drink your beer and leave me alone. What might or might not happen to me has nothing to do with you." Impatiently she moved away toward the waves lapping the hard-packed sand of the beach.

"Pete, go on back to the boat," Rhyder ordered curtly. "I'll stay here and keep an eye on her."

As if she was a child, Gina thought wretchedly, and raced toward the waves, diving shallowly into the water to hide the mortification he made her feel. For several minutes she exerted herself to the limits of her physical ability. She had to force herself to settle into a less tiring stroke and edge closer to shore.

After her rash boast, she didn't want to become too exhausted to reach shallow water and thus need to have Rhyder rescue her. Only once did she glance toward the beach to see if he had strayed. He was there and Pete had gone. She remained in the water for as long as she could, wanting Rhyder to have a long watch.

Eventually her muscles began to tremble in protest and she turned toward shore. When her toe scraped the bottom, she stood up and waded in. Her gaze slid over him where he stood out of reach of the lapping waves. The wait hadn't improved the chiseled harshness of his impenetrable mask.

Ignoring him as best she could, Gina walked to where her towel lay. Exhausted, she wanted nothing more than to collapse on the sand, but it would reveal a weakness that she would rather Rhyder didn't see. She picked up the towel and began briskly rubbing her arms, aware that Rhyder hadn't moved, only half turned to watch her.

"You can leave now." Bitterness caused her voice to tremble slightly. "As you can see, I survived the solitary swim. And I would have whether you had been on watch or not!"

"At least I know you're safe," he snapped.

"No one appointed you my guardian, certainly not me." Gina glared, her eyes flashing a stormy green. "There isn't any more reason for you to stay, so why don't you go?"

He came striding toward her. "You're the rudest little brat I've ever met! What you need is a good spanking to teach you some manners and some respect for your elders!"

Gina stiffened. "Don't you dare touch me!"

She couldn't have provoked him more if she had waved a red cape in front of him. In the next second, he was swinging her off her feet and carrying her to a rocky boulder farther along the shore, oblivious to her swinging hands and kicking feet.

Gina struggled and cursed, calling him every name she could think of as he swung her over his knee. After a half-dozen well-aimed and hard blows had been administered, Rhyder let her go.

Tears streamed down Gina's cheeks, partly from pain but mostly from the ultimate humiliation. She was afraid that if she opened her mouth to hurl abuse at him, she would start crying. She sent him a baleful look and spun away, running and stumbling to where she had dropped her towel in the initial scuffle. She fell to her knees beside it, sobbing her heart out.

A shadow fell across her, long at first, then shortening as Rhyder knelt beside her, but she couldn't stop crying, the sobs hiccuping from her chest. His hand touched the curve of her shoulder.

"I'm sorry, Gina," he murmured in a low voice.

"Leave me alone," she demanded through gritted teeth, and drew away from his hand.

"Dammit, Gina, I don't blame you for hating me because of what I did." His hand settled again on her shoulder, but this time in a grip she couldn't elude. Rhyder turned her around and drew her against his chest. She was too physically and mentally exhausted to struggle as he smoothed her wet hair with his fingers, nestling her head near the curve of his throat. "I'm sorry, Gina. I'm sorry." His mouth moved against her hair.

Even though she hated him, Gina sought the soothing comfort of his embrace. The racking sobs stopped inside the circle of his arms, reduced to sighing gasps. She lifted her head slightly as his mouth touched her temples, his breath warm against her skin. His lips encountered the first trace of tears along her cheekbone and Rhyder began kissing them away.

His hand curved along her slender throat, turning her face toward him. She seemed to stop breathing, not needing air as long as he continued exploring every inch of her face. When his mouth closed over her parted lips, she could taste the saltiness of her own tears in his kiss. The pressure of his hand near the small of her back arched her toward him.

Through the wetness of her swimsuit she could feel the solid beat of his heart. The mahogany hardness of his chest flattened her breasts. Where once there had been only the coldness of humiliation, a warmth began to spread.

Gina stopped passively accepting his kiss and began to return it. Her response deepened the kiss and the pressure of his mouth hardened in demanding possession. Gina answered as much as her limited experience allowed.

Rhyder lifted his head a fraction of an inch, their breaths mingling. "Open your lips, Gina," he instructed huskily.

She did, and his hard male lips claimed hers again, showing her the sensual fullness of a kiss between a man and a woman. Wildfire raced through her veins at his exploration. Her bones seemed to melt with the heat he was generating inside of her.

His weight was pressing her backward. It didn't ease, not even when gritty sand was beneath her shoulder blades. The heat of his sun-warmed body seemed to induce a languor that lifted her to a dreamlike state.

Tangy ocean salt clung to his skin, mixing with his musky male scent to make an intoxicating aroma. Her hands spread over the rippling, hard muscles of his back and shoulders, trying to evoke the same pleasure his stroking caress was giving her.

The knot of her swimsuit halter was digging into the back of her neck, an uncomfortable lump in an otherwise satisfying bed. She moved against Rhyder in relief when his exploring fingers encountered it and loosened it, pulling the straps away.

When Rhyder dragged his mouth from hers to explore the slender column of her throat, she felt a giddiness she had never previously experienced. She tipped her head back to expose every inch for his inspection.

Delicious shivers danced over her skin as he roughly nibbled at the lobe of her ear, then trailed over the sensitive cord to investigate the pulsing vein in her neck.

A thousand sensations assaulted her mind when he pushed the top of her swimsuit away and his hand glided over the curve of her breast. Fleetingly it occurred to Gina to protest against this liberty, but the firm, yet gentle caress of his hand erased her momentary apprehensions.

His warm mouth left the hollow of her throat, drawn to the pointed thrust of her breast. Primitive desire exploded within her at his possession of this previously private area. The fierceness of the emotion nearly overwhelmed her but Gina fought her way out of the whirlpool of uncontrolled passion, stiffening in fear at the wanton longings his fiery touch was arousing.

Immediately Rhyder shifted his attention to her lips. His burning kiss led her back to the whirlpool and reassured her she had nothing to fear in the drowning eddy of passion. Again her flesh became pliant to his touch, her limbs boneless. The moment of resistance had been conquered masterfully.

As her fingers started to curl into the wavy thickness of his black hair, Rhyder ripped himself from her, rolling away, turning his back to her as he knelt sitting on his heels. For a stunned moment, Gina lay where he had left her, staring dazedly at his slumped shoulders and bent head. She could see the effort he was making to try to control his erratic breathing.

"Rhyder?" She murmured his name in confusion and scooted into a half-sitting position.

Her trembling legs were curled to the side. She drew the top of her swimsuit over her nakedness, holding it in place with a shaking hand, and started to move toward him.

He either sensed her intention or heard her movement. "Don't come near me." His taut voice trembled huskily, but the tone was unmistakably commanding.

"Why?" she whispered, in a mute appeal to have him make her understand.

He raked a hand through the side of his hair

and answered roughly, "If you have any sense,
you'll leave me alone for a minute."

"But—"

·"Fix your swimming suit," ordered Rhyder, as
if giving her something to do.

Shakily Gina did as she was told. Her rounded
gaze of uncertain green· never left the point
between his shoulder blades. The wet straps of
her swimsuit weren't cooperating with her efforts
to tie them together, but Gina didn't really care.

"Did I . . . did I do something wrong?" she
asked hesitantly, betraying her youth and inex-
perience as she tried to find out why Rhyder had
so abruptly terminated the embrace.

There was a slight movement of his head in a
negative answer. "*You* didn't do anything
wrong,," he said in a sigh heavy with self-disgust.

"Then what is it?"

"What is it?" Rhyder laughed harshly as he
turned to look at her over his shoulder.

He stared at her ·for a long moment. His
savagely taunting laughter ended at the sight of
her. Gina didn't realize that the effects of his
lovemaking were still in her face. Her lips were
parted and sensually swollen by his possessive
kisses. In the bewildered green of her eyes, there
was still a fiery glow of desire. The softness of
surrender was in her features.

His eyes darkened to a midnight blue. For a
moment Gina thought he was going to gather
her again into his crushing embrace, but a mahogany mask stole over his features, carving
them with hardness.

A series of fluidly combined movements turned him to face her as he rose to his feet, his hands gripping her arms to draw her with him. She would have swayed against him, but iron muscles kept her an arm's length away.

"Don't you want me, Rhyder?" she asked, not meaning the question in a carnal way.

A muscle twitched in his jaw. He released her and bent to retrieve her towel from the sand. "You shouldn't ask such questions, Gina," he growled with taut control.

A crimson heat stained her cheeks as she realized what she had asked. Then, crazily, she knew she had to hear him say that she did attract him sexually, man to woman. She lowered her head, ignoring the towel he held out to her.

"Do you?" she persisted quietly in a strained voice.

"Dammit!" He reached out to jerk her a foot closer to him.

Her face lifted to gaze at the impatient anger in his expression. Rhyder's attention became focused on her mouth. The parted softness of her lips was an irresistible lure. He pulled her within an inch of his own.

"Dammit, yes," Rhyder muttered brokenly, and claimed her lips once more as his personal possession.

His arms circled her in an iron band to crush her against the naked wall of his chest. The sun-bleached hair on his legs chafed the smooth skin of her thighs as he molded her to his length. Arched roughly against him, Gina felt the thrust of his male hardness and, for the first time in her young life, knew the answering, primitive ache within herself.

With a muffled groan, Rhyder pushed her away, shoving the beach towel into her hands. Gina didn't protest this time. She was shaken by the discovery that his touch could completely make her lose control, something she thought happened only in romantic novels. The realization was sobering.

"Go home, Gina," Rhyder ordered tersely. "Go home to your grandfather before . . . ." He clamped his mouth shut without completing the sentence.

"I . . . ." She wanted to say something. She didn't know what. She didn't need any pictures drawn for her.

Rhyder turned away, massaging the back of his neck. "For God's sake, don't say any more," he said thickly.

Bowing her head, raven hair falling across her cheek in a silken tangle, Gina took a step toward the rocky path leading from the beach, then hesitated.

She glanced back at him. "I'm sorry," she murmured, without really understanding for what.

"You're sorry!" Rhyder breathed out roughly, the blue lance of his gaze piercing her. "The disgusting part is that I'm not!"

A cold chill ran down her spine. Her knuckles were white from the death grip on the beach towel. A chasm seemed to be widening between them and it frightened her. "Will I . . . see you again?" she whispered.

"Not if I can help it," he muttered.

"Rhyder." She issued a broken plea for him not to mean that.

"Are you so young that you don't realize what's happening?" He tipped his head to one side, the line of his mouth uncompromising and grim.

"I don't care." The tortured words were torn from her throat.

"You damned well should," snapped Rhyder.

Gina flinched. "Are you leaving?"

A heavy sigh broke from him and he paused before answereing. "Not right away," he admitted grudgingly.

"Then I will see you again?" she persisted in breathless hope.

"I suppose it's inevitable."

Rhyder walked away toward the ocean waves. He didn't look back as Gina slipped on her sandals and took the path up the headlands. She felt caught in a vacuum, between boundless love and despair.

CHAPTER THREE

"ONE OF YOUR FRIENDS left today," Nate Gaynes announced blandly.

"Really?" Uninterestedly, Gina stabbed at a pea on her plate.

"Aye," her grandfather nodded. His hair had once been as dark as hers, but age had liberally streaked it with iron gray. The years hadn't dimmed the perception of his eyes. They gleamed now keenly at Gina across the table. "The coast guard got ahold of him this mornin'. There was some emergency in his family and he flew home."

"He?" Until that moment Gina hadn't been paying attention to what her grandfather was saying.

Now it was undivided. Initially she had thought he was talking about a school friend going off on vacation, but that wasn't whom he had meant.

"That's what I said." He bent over his plate.

"From the *Sea Witch*?"

"Aye."

"Which one left?" Gina held her breath.

"The sunny-haired one."

Relief washed through her. "That's Pete."

"That could have been his name," he conceded.

Gina fell silent, the possible implication of her grandfather's announcement racing through her mind. Since the afternoon on the beach, she had seen Rhyder on three different occasions. Each time Pete had been present, unknowingly acting as a chaperon. Rhyder had said little to her. Most of the conversation had been between Gina and Pete.

The meetings hadn't been all that satisfying, although a couple of times Gina had caught Rhyder watching her as she talked to Pete. Naked desire had burned in his eyes, only to be quickly veiled when he became aware that she had noticed. Not once had he attempted to be alone with her or indicated a wish to be.

But Pete had left. He wouldn't be there anymore to keep them apart. Hope flamed with new vigor. Another thought occurred to her before the renewed fire got out of control.

"What about Rhyder?" she asked suddenly. "Will he be leaving?"

"I shouldn't think he'd be goin' anytime soon, unless he's a fool. Strikes me he'd be smart enough to hire him another deckhand before fightin' his way up to Boston. Either that or wait for this Pete to come back, if he's comin' back." Nate Gaynes leaned back in his chair and took a pipe out of his pocket.

Silently Gina agreed that Rhyder wasn't a fool. It wouldn't be easy for him to find a deckhand, either. Most of the men in the immediate vicinity were already employed. It would take at least a couple of days, if he were lucky, to find someone to replace Pete.

Gina glowed with the knowledge that she'd be able to see Rhyder again—alone. There wasn't any way he could prevent it. And she believed that secretly he didn't want to, not really.

"You're sure lookin' happy as a clam about somethin'," her grandfather observed, holding a match to his pipe and puffing until the bowl of tobacco glowed.

Gina flushed slightly and began stacking the supper dishes. "Really, gramps, I don't know what you're talking about," she shrugged off-handedly.

"Harrumph!" he snorted in disbelief. "You've been moonin' around this house for the better part of a week. The last person I remember behavin' that way was your daddy. It was back when he was seein' your mother before they was married. Trouble was, she was seein' the Wilkes boy, too. He was actin' about the same way you been."

"I'm surprised you can remember back that far, gramps." Gina kept her face averted as she teased him in an attempt to change the subject.

"I do." The pipe was clamped between his teeth, the fragrant aroma filling the kitchen. "I notice you ain't denyin' it."

"Denying what?" She tried to sound blank and indifferent.

"That you admire this Rhyder feller."

"What are you talking about?" Gina carried

the dishes to the sink and turned on the taps to draw the dishwater.

But Nate Gaynes ignored her question. "He's a good bit older than you. You realize that, don't you?"

"You were eleven years older than grandma," she pointed out, adding the dish soap.

He ignored that comment, too. "And you don't know how he is with women. With his money and background, females probably fall all over him. It ain't the kind of thing that would make him exactly respectful. He's probably used to takin' what he wants and throwin' it away when he don't care about it anymore."

"You don't know that for sure," Gina protested lamely.

"You have to admit he isn't a 'please-and-thank-you' man." Gina didn't respond to that observation. More pipe smoke filled the air as her grandfather paused before continuing. "There's another thing. He'll be leavin' soon. Chances are he won't be comin' back this way, maybe never."

"What are you trying to say, grandfather?" she demanded stiffly, forsaking her more affectionate term of address at his calm but disheartening reasoning. "Are you trying to tell me I shouldn't see him again?"

"No," he drawled slowly. "I ain't a-tellin' you what to do nor what not to do. I just don't want you to go gettin' carried away by somethin' that probably don't have a snowball's chance of amountin' to anything."

"Yes, gramps," Gina submitted.

But his words only filled her with a sense of desperation. She simply had to see Rhyder. Everything would be all right if only she could see him again. Then her grandfather's warnings would prove empty.

It wasn't until the following day that she was able to see him. He was on the deck of his boat polishing the brass fittings when she approached. At the sound of her footsteps on the wooden dock, he glanced up, nodded, and returned his attention to his work.

"Hello, Gina," Rhyder greeted her smoothly.

"Hi. You're working hard, I see," she returned.

"Trying to." He smiled at her briefly, but continued with his task.

"I heard Pete had to fly home yesterday," Gina said.

"That's right." Rhyder straightened. "His sister was in a serious automobile accident."

"Was she hurt very badly?"

"Not as badly as they thought at first," he answered, glancing at the gold watch on his wrist. "He phoned me last night to let me know."

"Is he coming back?" she inquired, trying to conceal how deeply interested she was in his answer.

His mouth tightened. "Unless Jill, his sister, develops complications, he'll be back at the end of the week."

"You're on your own until then, huh?" She smiled with difficulty, crossing her fingers that he might say something about spending time with her.

Rhyder shrugged and turned away. "I don't mind."

She bit into her lip, nibbling briefly at is softness. "If you get tired of your own cooking, you can come have supper with gramps and me one night," she offered tentatively.

"Maybe." But he made it sound as if it were unlikely he would take her up on the invitation.

"Would you like some help polishing the brass?"

"I can manage."

The corners of her mouth sagged downward in bitter disappointment. Rhyder couldn't have made it plainer that he didn't want her around. The ocean green of her eyes became murky with despair, the thick fringe of her long lashes adding to their troubled darkness. She reached inside herself to extract a measure of pride.

"I won't keep you from your work, then," she declared, half-turned to leave.

There was a half-smothered oath from Rhyder, then, "Gina!" which drew her resentful glance. "If you want to make yourself useful, you can fix some coffee," he stated. Immediately a savage grimness entered his expression as if he was angry with himself for making the suggestion.

Gina hesitated, stiffly aware that he was regretting his offer. She wouldn't be indulged, like a child. "You're very self-sufficient, Rhyder. I'm sure you can fix it yourself."

His look hardened. "I asked you." He turned his back to her and resumed his polishing.

He wasn't the type to beg her. The decision was hers and she would be a fool to pass up the chance for his company. There might not be another. Swallowing her pride, Gina stepped aboard.

Rhyder didn't turn around to look at her as he said, "You know where everything is. Bring it on deck when it's ready."

Bitterness welled inside her. Sure, Gina thought resentfully as she stiffly descended the steps to the galley, bring it on deck where they would be in full view of everyone at the harbor. Instead of one chaperon, Pete, they would have a dozen or more.

She obeyed his edict and dutifully carried the mugs on deck when the coffee was done. Gina had half expected Rhyder to continue his work and ignore her. It was a pleasant surprise when he set down his polishing rag to take the coffee.

While it cooled to a drinkable temperature, they talked about sailing, the coast of Maine, the weather, and various other inconsequential things. His air of friendliness enveloped Gina in a warm feeling of pleasure. All her earlier resentment was gone.

"It's going to be a warm night tonight," Rhyder commented.

She gazed skyward, noting the high cirrus clouds moving in. Mare's tails, she thought, meant rain tomorrow, but she didn't say that.

"Yes," she agreed with his remark, redirecting

her gaze to his strong, carved profile. "It will be a perfect night for a moonlight swim."

His gaze sliced to her, then shifted to his brown mug. There was a subtle change in his manner. "It probably will be," he conceded noncommittally.

"Are you doing anything special tonight?" Gina asked boldly.

"No, nothing special." There was a visible hardness to the line of his jaw.

"Well?" Gina tipped her head to one side in a flash of impatience. "Do I have to ask you to take me on a moonlight swim?"

"Gina," Rhyder began, breathing in her name with vague irritation, "why don't you invite some nice boy your own age? Someone who'll stroll along the beach with you and hold your hand, maybe steal a kiss or two while he shows you the stars. What you want is a harmless little flirtation." He looked at her long and hard. "I'm a man, Gina; I don't play those innocent roles anymore. You should be seeing someone who doesn't want to make love to you every time he takes you in his arms."

"Maybe that's what I want you to do," she breathed in helpless longing.

"Don't be deliberately provocative, Gina," Rhyder ordered sharply, but the smoldering darkness of his blue eyes was involuntarily running over her curved figure, belying the adult indifference he was trying to project. "If you had any brains in that beautiful head of yours, you would avoid me like the plague," he finished grimly.

"Do you really think I'm beautiful?" Gina murmured. Only his backhanded compliment registered in her mind.

"You know you are." His gaze locked onto hers, almost unwillingly, as if compelled by a force he fiercely resented. "Those eyes of yours, like the emerald depths of the ocean, luring a man on until . . . ."

He broke off in midsentence, taking a step away from her toward the railing. He stood there with his legs slightly apart, braced to the gentle roll of the boat, and gazed at the limitless stretch of ocean.

Rhyder's words thrilled Gina to the very marrow of her being because they were so reluctantly issued and had ended the instant he realized what he was revealing.

Confident now of her attraction, Gina moved to his side. She stood at a right angle to him. "No one has ever said anything like that to me before," she commented artlessly.

Nothing in the carved mahogany of his features indicated he had heard her. He seemed like a statue of some mythological sun god. Gina was overwhelmed by an urge to touch him and make sure he was flesh and blood, not some figment of her imagination.

This compulsion carried her hand to his sun-browned arm. The muscles contracted at the touch of her fingers, rippling in reaction. His head jerked downward to stare at the hand lightly resting on his arm. Finally his gaze lifted to her face.

An impenetrable mask covered his features, but the blazing passion in his eyes jolted through her. Rhyder turned slowly to face her and Gina's hand dropped to her side. He towered above her, vitally masculine, so close that she had to tip her head back to see his face. Scant inches separated their bodies, yet neither of them attempted to bridge the short distance.

A wild pagan song was drumming through her pulse. Flames of passion engulfed her, licking her nerve ends until her skin burned. He was seducing her, making love to her in his mind. And the spiritual union was as real to Gina as it would have been if her flesh had actually experienced his possession.

When the soundless music playing between them rose to a crescendo, they strained toward each other without breaking the invisible barrier of inches. Rhyder seemed to strive for control.

"Gina." His voice was low and charged by the emotion-packed minutes. "Can you read my mind, too?"

"Yes," she answered weakly.

The spell that gripped them was broken by the long breath Rhyder exhaled, a sound of angry exasperation. He widened the distance between them, an expressionless mask stealing over his face.

"I think you'd better leave," he told her levelly.

Gina was stung by his withdrawal. "After I've

cleared away the coffee things," she insisted stubbornly.

"Don't bother. I'll take care of them after you've gone," responded Rhyder in the same calm tone he had used before.

"You always seem to be telling me to leave," she sighed in frustration.

"I'm just trying to do what's right," he said with faint tautness.

"Right for whom?" Gina challenged. "For me? I think I'm a better judge of that."

He controlled the impatience that flashed across his face and said firmly, but gently, "Gina, I don't want to argue with you. This time you will go quietly without involving us in some harsh disagreement. We're both on edge," he breathed in, "and it isn't going to get any easier."

"All right." Gina submitted reluctantly to his logic and left with a simple goodbye.

THAT EVENING a rising, lopsided moon found Gina wandering along the quiet beach. Although Rhyder had not indicated that he would be meeting her for a moonlight swim, Gina had come on the chance he'd be there.

But the sands were deserted. There was only the soft rustle of nightlife and the subdued rush of waves onto the beach. For nearly an hour she waited, staring at the moon. It was almost full, looking as if someone had chiseled a silvery arc from its circle. Finally she returned home.

By the following afternoon, the portent of yesterday's mare's tail and mackerel sky had come true. It was raining steadily, without any sign of letup. The weather kept her grandfather at home. Gina was trapped there, as well, spending most of the rainy hours restlessly prowling the house trying to think of a valid excuse to leave.

She wanted to see Rhyder, but she didn't want her grandfather to know. It was the first time in her sixteen years that she could ever remember wanting to keep something from him. The subsequent guilt made her all the more tense.

The cloud-covered sky brought an early darkness. At half-past eight Nate Gaynes was dozing in his big armchair. From past experience Gina knew he would probably sleep there until after midnight before rousing to go to his bed.

All day long the events of the previous day and the comments Rhyder had made had been running through her mind. A decision had formed, one that Gina didn't want to think about in case she lost her courage. With her grandfather sleeping in the chair, she had the chance to put it into action.

Quietly she slipped out of the house and ran through the steadily falling raindrops to the harbor. Her heart was hammering madly against her ribs when she reached the dock. A light gleamed in the darkness from the port window of the *Sea Witch II*. Rhyder was there.

Pausing only for an instant, she hopped aboard and darted down the steps to knock at the galley door. It was opened almost instantly by Rhyder, who had probably risen at the sound of footsteps on deck. He stared at her for a stunned moment before becoming aware of the falling rain. He took hold of a wet wrist and drew her inside.

"What are you doing out in this downpour?" he muttered as he shut the door behind her.

"I wanted to see you." There was lilt of urgency in her voice.

He stared at her for another second, taking in the cotton blouse and slacks that were plastered against her skin, water dripping on the galley floor. More water trickled down her forehead from her rain-soaked hair.

"You're drenched to the skin," he accused her in irritation. "You should have worn a raincoat."

His words made her feel like a straggly kitten half-drowned by a downpour. "I know I should have," she admitted, shivering more from her cool reception than from the damp. "I forgot all about the rain when I made up my mind to come."

His mouth was compressed grimly for a minute. "Wait here," he ordered. "I'll get a towel or something to dry you off."

As he disappeared down the narrow corridor, Gina hesitated for a split second, then started stripping off the wet clothes until they lay in a watery puddle on the floor. Self-consciously she crossed her arms in front of her at the sound of Rhyder's return.

Ducking his ebony head to enter the galley area, he came to an abrupt halt at the sight of her. A folded blanket was in his hand. Gina's teeth began to chatter uncontrollably. It wasn't from cold. She was frightened by the shamelessness of her own behavior where Rhyder was concerned.

His features were half in shadow, the angular planes revealing nothing. She sought the clear blue of his eyes. They mirrored the image of a slender girlchild. Words tumbled from her tongue to dispel the image.

"I want you to make love to me, Rhyder." Her voice was thin, betraying the taut state of her nerves. "That's why I came. No one has ever made me feel the way you do when you kiss me. And I remember what you said yesterday about being a man a-and not playing those innocent games of kissing and holding hands. It's true about you, I know—about being a man, I mean, and wanting more from a woman than just kisses. I want more than that, too. I—"

"Gina—" he began, his head moving to the side in a hopeless gesture.

"No, let me finish," she rushed in. "I know you'll be leaving sometime, probably before the summer is over. I might not ever see you again." She breathed in shakily, the blood roaring in her ears. "But I love you, Rhyder, and I want to belong to you completely, even if it is only for a little while. I swear I won't ask any more than that from you. I just want you to love me."

Her voice trailed off lamely as he walked slowly toward her. The shadowy light from the single lamp didn't illuminate his expression. She searched with pathetic eagerness for some indication of his answer. When he stopped in front of her, his mouth was curved in a tender smile, but it told her nothing.

His unreadable gaze never left her upturned face as he unfolded the blanket and drew it gently around her shoulders. Gina trembled at the touch of the soft woolen material against her naked skin. He crossed the ends securely in front of her, tucking it under her chin and holding it shut with one hand.

"Oh, Gina . . . ." He murmured her name in a sigh that almost sounded sad.

Her chin quivered. "Please, Rhyder, don't send me away," she begged. "I couldn't stand it."

"Someday—" he tenderly brushed a damp strand of hair from her cheek "—a nice young man will come along and you'll marry him in a big church wedding, walking down the aisle in a lace gown with your grandfather beside you. And you'll probably have a houseful of kids with green eyes and dark hair. That's when it will stop hurting and you'll look back on this moment and be glad that I told you to go home."

"No!" Gina protested with a sobbing cry.

"Go home, Gina," Rhyder insisted quietly. "Go home and wait until you're grown up. Save all that love for the right man when he comes along."

"I love you," she pleaded desperately.

"No." He shook his head. "I've only awakened the woman in you. Now you want to experiment, to discover what it's all about. You picked me because I was at the right place at the right time in your life, but I'm the wrong man."

The pain shattering through her body was too great to be borne. "You're nothing but a hypocrite!" she hurled at him through her tears. "How dare you preach at me! I hate you! Do you hear?" she screamed hoarsely. "I hate you!"

But her violently hurled rejection of Rhyder didn't hurt him as she had wanted it to, and she choked back the bitter anguish. His fingers released the blanket and she pivoted away, clutching the ends with one hand and grabbing for the door with the other. As she pulled it open, his hand gripped her shoulder to stop her.

"Gina, for God's sake, don't—"

She twisted away from his hand and dashed up the steps. Tears were streaming so rapidly from her eyes that she didn't even notice the rain. She was only aware of Rhyder mounting the steps behind her and she ran as if fleeing from the devil.

At some point in her headlong flight, Gina realized that he was no longer behind her, but she didn't slow her racing strides. She was too numbed with pain to feel the slippery sharpness of the gravel beneath her bare feet or the sharp whip of the wet blanket against her legs.

There seemed to be no air left in her lungs, but still she ran, pursued by shame and humiliation at the fool she had made of herself.

The light of her home gleamed ahead and she used the last of her strength to reach the door, flinging it open and stumbling inside. Heaving sobs shook her shoulders as she pushed the door closed. She leaned weakly against it, needing its solid support.

"Gina!" Her grandfather's astonished voice startled her. "What happened to you, child?"

Still gasping with uncontrolled sobs, she tried to focus her tear-blurred gaze on the spare figure standing near the entryway. Then she realized the blanket had slipped from one shoulder, exposing the bare curve of a breast.

Quickly she covered it, but it was too late. Fresh waves of humiliation swamped her as she remembered the wet pile of her clothes on the galley floor.

"Where have you been?" Nate Gaynes demanded in a steely voice that sent a shaft of fear through Gina. "Who were you with?"

She opened her mouth, but no words would come out, only more sobs. What must he be thinking of her, she thought wretchedly as she stared at the graying pallor in her grandfather's face.

"You were with that Rhyder feller, weren't you?" he said stiffly.

Gina nodded. Bowing her head, she cried harder. "I'm s-so ashamed," she sobbed.

He walked to her, a weathered hand reaching out, but Gina couldn't accept his offer of comfort. Not after the way she had shamed him by her actions.

With a broken cry of pain she ran past him to the stairs, racing up them to her room. She slammed the door behind her and threw herself

across the quilted spread on her bed. She heard
his footstep on the stairs, but someone pounded
on the front door. Her grandfather hesitated
before turning back to answer it.

The walls of the old house were hardly sound-
proof. Gina's heart stopped beating when she
heard Rhyder's voice below. He had followed
her!

"Did Gina come back here?" he demanded.

Her grandfather must have nodded his answer. "You're just the man I wanted to see," he
said ominously.

"I've brought your granddaughter's shoes and
clothes. I know how it must look to you, but I
believe I can explain." Rhyder's tone was respectful, but he didn't sound intimidated by the
situation or her grandfather.

There was a pause during which, Gina
guessed, her grandfather was sizing up the stranger. In a slow, drawling voice, he said, "We'll go
through to the kitchen and have our talk there."

CHAPTER FOUR

THE KITCHEN WAS directly below Gina's bedroom, and the floor register permitted her to hear
what was being said. She was shivering again
and threw off the wet blanket to slip beneath the
covers of her bed.

Shutting her eyes tightly, she tried to block out
the whole miserable scene, but she couldn't shut
her ears to the voices below. More slow, hot tears
squeezed through her wet lashes.

"I could do with a shot of whiskey," her
grandfather said. "You?"

For a while there was only the drumming rain
on the roof. Glasses clinked as they were set on
the kitchen table, followed by the thud of a
bottle, the one kept for "medicinal purposes" on
the top shelf of the cupboard.

"I knew she was taken with you. I probably
should have forbidden her to see you, but I was
afraid of sweetenin' the excitement." There was
a thread of weariness in her grandfather's sigh
that made Gina feel all the more wretched. But
there was no sign of it when he added sharply,
"You knew she was only sixteen, didn't you?"

Rhyder swore softly. "She told me she was
seventeen."

"Not until August," Nate Gaynes har-rumphed. "But you believed her?"

"Your granddaughter is sixteen going on twenty," he declared grimly.

"That may be, but she's still a minor in the eyes of the law," her grandfather pointed out. "So maybe you'd just better tell me what did happen tonight and how my granddaughter's clothes came to be in your possession while she was running through the streets stark naked except for a blanket flappin' in the wind."

Clearly and concisely Rhyder sketched the night's happenings, not dwelling long on Gina's impassioned plea for him to make love to her. Gina wished she could fall asleep and never wake up again.

When he had concluded his explanation, there was a long pause. The bottle thudded again on the table, no doubt after refilling the glasses.

"And you expect me to believe this was all her idea?" Nate's quiet voice was piercing. "It couldn't be that you suggested it and she got cold feet at the last minute and ran away?"

"I swear I didn't lay a hand on her." Rhyder's tone didn't vary in its pitch, conviction running firmly through his words.

Gina turned her face into the pillow, shame scorching through her veins. Her grandfather must despise her. He had trusted her and she had let him down.

"And I don't suppose you ever did anything to make Gina think that you might be wantin' to bed her?" came the quiet challenge.

This time Rhyder hesitated. "I might have, yes," he said finally.

"You *might* have?" Her grandfather demanded a more definite answer.

"All right, I did," he admitted grudgingly.

"A girl doesn't get that kind of an idea from a man who's only stolen a kiss or two," her grandfather stated.

"I . . . did step out of line a couple of times." Self-anger sharpened his reluctant response.

But it didn't ease Gina's humiliation to hear him concede that he was partially to blame for her behavior that night. She simply buried her head deeper in the pillow, trying to muffle their voices.

"I'm glad to hear you admit that," Nate Gaynes declared, faintly triumphant. "Now maybe we can get down to some serious talking."

The bottle thudded on the tabletop for the third time. Gina pulled the pillow over her head and began sobbing into the sheet-covered mattress. She couldn't bear to listen to them discussing her as if she were a child. It was the final humiliation. The tears couldn't begin to ease the agony of self-torture, but they flowed from a bottomless well.

Time was measureless. Seconds seemed minutes. Minutes seemed hours. And Gina cried for an eternity. Several times she heard voices raised in anger from the kitchen below, but they only served to increase her torment.

Once she heard Rhyder angrily state, "Dammit, man! You're asking the impossible!" Her grandfather's reply was muffled.

And Gina possessed no curiosity to know specifically what they were discussing. She knew it concerned her. More than that she didn't want to know. At last her sobs were reduced to dry, hacking sounds. Emotional exhaustion carried her into sleep.

A knock on the door wakened her. Gina rolled over, fighting through the drugged stupor that made her feel leaden and lifeless. She blinked her heavy lids and became immediately conscious of her nakedness beneath the covers. A tortured moan of remembrance broke from her lips.

The sound prompted another knock at her door. Gina stared at the wooden door, wanting to order whoever was on the other side to go away, but no sound could get through the constricted muscles in her throat. She wished there was a lock on the door so no one could ever enter. She didn't want to see anybody ever again.

The door was opened without her permission and the gently smiling face of her grandfather greeted her from the hallway. Gina turned her head away as he walked into the room, carrying a tray. The covers were up around her neck and she didn't move when he stopped beside the bed.

"Sit up, Gina," he told her with forced cheerfulness. "I'm treatin' you to breakfast in bed."

She couldn't sit up. She was too self-conscious of her unclothed state. Why hadn't she put some clothes on last night, she wondered bitterly. Then she wouldn't be embarrassing herself in this way.

"I don't want anything," she mumbled, refusing to look at him.

"There's some hot chocolate here, toast and jelly."

He was trying to tempt her again as if she were a child. Gina turned her face deeper into the pillow. "Please, I don't want anything," she repeated hoarsely.

Her grandfather set the tray on the stand beside her bed and turned to her huddled figure. He sat down on the edge of the bed, a weathered hand smoothing the tangle of black hair from her cheek.

"I know you feel badly, Gina." He tried to comfort her.

Her lashes curved into each other as she pressed them tightly closed. "I wish I could die," she whispered.

"That's a bit drastic, don't you think," he smiled.

"I don't care." Gina caught back a sob.

"Now you know you don't mean that," he insisted gently. "Everything will work out all right. You'll see."

"How can it? You must be so ashamed of me." She felt as small as a flea.

"Last night—" his gnarled hand rested on her hair "—when you went to him, you went because you loved him, didn't you?" her grandfather questioned.

"Y-yes." That's what she had thought. Now she hated him and she hated herself.

"Love, and things done in love, are not something to be ashamed of, child. I'm not condoning what you did, but I understand," he told her.

"You don't understand." Her head moved restively beneath his touch. "I don't see how I can face anyone again."

"You'll soon change your mind about that. After you and Rhyder are married—"

"Married?" Gina stared at him, eyes rounded, all her senses alert. "But I'm not going to marry Rhyder," she protested when she could breathe again.

"Yes, you are," her grandfather nodded. "We arranged it all last night. It will be a quiet and simple ceremony. I'm afraid there isn't time for something more elaborate."

"But I'm not going to marry him!" What little color there had been in her face was gone.

"It's the only sensible solution," he soothed.

"No!" Gina turned away, frightened and appalled by what he was suggesting. "He doesn't want me."

"He has agreed to marry you," her grandfather reminded her.

"Well, I won't marry him!"

"Gina, you must." There was strain in his voice as he tried to convince her.

"Why?" she challenged. "Why must I?" She glanced at him angrily and saw the pain in his eyes.

"Do you think no one saw you running from the harbor last night?" he sighed sadly.

Crimson heat spread over her cheeks. "Did someone see me?" Her chin trembled.

Nate Gaynes nodded reluctantly. "A few 'well-meaning' friends stopped over this morning to tell me about it, just in case I didn't know," he replied dryly.

"Oh, no!" Gina moaned. "But nothing happened," she argued weakly.

"There are many who wouldn't believe that. Mostly because they wouldn't want to," he explained. "Their waggin' tongues wouldn't give you any peace, girl."

She was ruined. No decent boy would look at her now. The tale would be spread all over the community. Everyone would know, if they didn't already. Her every action would be subject to their censure after this. The only way she could eradicate the strain on her reputation would be to marry her supposed partner in sin.

It wasn't fair, she thought bitterly. But people in small communities were notorious for minding everybody's business but their own. It was bad enough for herself, but her grandfather would be included in the backlash.

Surely there had to be a way out of the situation that didn't involve marrying Rhyder. She hated him. After the way he had humiliated her, she couldn't marry him. What other choice was there?

"Why couldn't we move away?" she asked suddenly.

"Move away!" Her grandfather was plainly taken aback by the suggestion, a frown darkening his forehead.

"No," Gina sighed, "I guess we couldn't."

It wouldn't be fair, either, to ask her grandfather to give up his home, the one he had shared with his beloved wife and his children; and the lobster traps he had hauled all his life; and his friends. She stared at the ceiling.

"I won't marry him," she repeated with conviction.

"It's all settled," he stated crisply. "If everyone is going to wait to see if you're up a stump, then I want you married while they're doing it."

"I am not pregnant," Gina protested. "I couldn't be!"

An arched eyebrow asked her who would believe that. She knew the answer was a rare few. She sank her teeth into her lower lip to keep from crying out her frustration. She felt trapped.

IN THE END, Gina did as her grandfather asked. She didn't see Rhyder until the marriage ceremony. Not that she had cared, she tried to tell herself. She kept insisting silently that she didn't want to see him. She guessed her grandfather had shrewdly kept Rhyder away in case she should say something that would be contrary to his wishes.

Rhyder's expression had been bland as he stood beside her in front of the minister. He had spoken the vows clearly and without emotion. Nothing in his eyes had revealed his inner opinion of the marriage; he had rarely glanced at her. When they had been pronounced man and wife, he had brushed her lips coolly.

During the congratulations from the handful of people invited to attend, he had dutifully remained at her side. But Gina had noticed with growing irritation the way he avoided touching her. His aloofness was cutting. Her grandfather had assured her that Rhyder was very willing to marry her. Gina thought he had a very strange way of showing it.

A token amount of rice had marked their departure from the church. Rhyder had brushed the few grains from the shoulder of his jacket before sliding behind the wheel of the car. Gina had plucked one from her hair and was rolling it between her thumb and forefinger.

They had driven for nearly twenty minutes and not once had he spoken to her. The silence was stretching like a rubber band, each minute increasing its tautness.

Impatiently Gina tossed the grain of rice to the floor. "This is impossible!" she snapped.

His gaze slid to her, brief and sweeping, yet his aura remained decidedly remote. "What is?"

Her mouth was compressed tightly, her nerves gratingly on edge. "All of this," she declared with encompassing bitterness. "Why are we going to a hotel anyway?"

"It's our wedding night. Have you forgotten?" Behind the dryness, there was a hint of a jeer.

"How could I?" she breathed tightly. "We

could just as easily have gone to your boat instead of this."

"Your grandfather wanted you to have a proper honeymoon." A corner of his mouth lifted cynically.

"I don't particularly care," Gina retorted.

"Neither do I."

"Then why are you going through with it?" she demanded throwing him a cold look.

His profile was chiseled against a golden sunset, its lines hard and unyielding. This indomitable person was her husband. The thought chilled her.

"Your grandfather has a way of getting what he wants." There was a slight tightening of the muscles in his jaw, although his voice was level and composed.

"That almost sounds as if you're frightened of him," Gina taunted.

Cool blue eyes held her gaze for an instant before Rhyder returned his attention to the highway. A dark, forbidding light had been burning in their depths.

"He's a shrewd man," was his noncommittal answer.

Gina tipped her head to one side, her green eyes narrowing at the insult she sensed behind his remark. "Why did you say that?" She studied him warily.

The creases at the corners of his mouth deepened in a humorless expression. "He arranged the marriage, didn't he?"

"Yes." Gina's first thought was of her stubborn resistance to the idea. "He wanted to save my reputation. It meant a great deal more to him than it did to me. That's the only reason why I married you," she told him flatly. "To save my reputation in the eyes of my grandfather's friends."

"I married you for the same reason," Rhyder inserted sardonically. "To save my reputation."

"That's a joke," she laughed shortly and with bitterness. "A man can do almost anything and not get into trouble. He can sow all the wild oats he wants and only a few will click their tongues. But a girl gets branded as a tramp. It isn't fair!"

"Nothing in life is fair," he said dryly. "A fact you'll discover as you grow up."

"Will you stop referring to me as if I were an infant!" Gina snapped. "I happen to be your wife."

"I'm not likely to forget it." Harsh and cold, his gaze pinned her, his lip curling, as he added, "*Mrs.* Owens."

Suddenly Gina was afraid. She didn't really know anything about this man sitting beside her. She didn't know if he had a family, what he did for a living, nothing. She sat back in her seat, trembling, and stared straight ahead.

"Y-your parents," she faltered, "do they know about me?"

"Not yet," he answered grimly.

A hotel sign blinked its neon lights ahead of them. Rhyder slowed the car to make the turn into the driveway. The night air was warm on her ıs he opened her car door, but Gina felt unaccountably cold.

The hand directing her into the lobby was not at all gentle. Her skin burned under the tight grip that wouldn't allow her to pull free.

Glancing around the richly furnished reception area, she tried to ignore the speculating look of the desk clerk. Vaguely she heard Rhyder mention something about reservations. Nausea gripped her stomach as her downcast gaze saw him write Mr. and Mrs. Rhyder Owens on the registration slip.

"Would you like the honeymoon suite, sir?" the clerk inquired somewhat suggestively, and Gina flushed in miserable embarrassment.

Rhyder flicked a hard, mocking glance in her direction and answered, "By all means," with something cruel in his tone.

Her ears were burning as the bellboy escorted them to their suite, carrying their few pieces of luggage. Gina discovered the conjecture and gossip of strangers was more unendurable than if it had come from people she had known all her life. She felt sickened by the ribald wink the bellboy had given Rhyder when he accepted his tip and left them in the room.

The scarlet-covered bed dominated the room. Gina walked stiffly to the window, wanting to ignore it. Her forehead felt clammy and she knew she had grown pale. Rhyder's gaze was on her. She could feel it prickling her spine.

"Have you eaten anything today?" He sounded like a parent and Gina gritted her teeth.

"Very little. Bridal nerves, I suppose," she tacked on bitterly.

"Would you like to go to the restaurant or shall ·I order something from room service?" Rhyder inquired politely and indifferently.

Her first instinct was to choose the restaurant, but the prospect of being the recipient of knowing looks from the hotel staff quickly made her reject it.

"Room service please," she answered stiffly. "And order lots of champagne. I feel like getting drunk."

"Don't try to be sophisticated, Gina," Rhyder snapped. "You can't carry it off."

Tension gnawed at her stomach. She pivoted to meet the hard glint of his eyes, cold blue steel that bored right through her. The proud lift of her dark head elevated her chin to a defiant angle.

"Are you ashamed of me?" Despite her bold challenge, she felt intimidated by the raw masculinity emanating from the dark-suited man standing only a few feet away. Her heart began beating in sharp, uneven thuds at the harsh twist of his mouth.

"What makes you ask that?" The bland question was not what she had been prepared for. Anger she would have expected, or snide sarcasm.

"Because you haven't told your parents about our marriage." Gina held her breath, frightened by the way she was trying to provoke his anger.

His eyes narrowed swiftly. "I will inform them

in my own time. We're married—which is, after all, what you wanted."

"It isn't what I wanted!" she choked.

"You're quite right," Rhyder agreed with an acid touch of irony. "You only wanted to conduct a sexual experiment. It's a pity you didn't think about that when you ran from the boat, or you wouldn't be paying the consequences now and neither of us would be in this mess."

Tears stung her eyelids. She turned back to the window so he wouldn't see. She didn't need his harsh reminder that her foolishness was to blame for the present situation. The scarlet carpet partially muffled his footsteps, but she was aware of him walking toward her and stiffened.

"Here's the room service menu." He thrust a printed paper toward her. "You can choose what you like," he said, curt and indifferent.

"It doesn't matter." Gina shifted her position to keep her back to him. "Order anything—I don't care."

"Very well." His patience was being stretched. She could hear it in his clipped tone. Rhyder turned away, muscles rippling tautly beneath the neatly tailored suit. "I'll order for you. You can freshen up while I phone."

Incensed by his patronizing inflection, Gina spun around. Emerald fire blazed in her eyes, made even brighter by a shimmer of tears.

"Why don't you just tell me to go wash my hands like a good little girl?" she stormed.

"That's enough, Gina!" His ominous warning lashed out like the flicking sting of a whip.

"What's the matter?" she taunted, without the slightest regard to his admonition. "Are you afraid I'm becoming hysterical?"

"I wouldn't be surprised," Rhyder said with quiet grimness, his temper severely checked. "You've used nearly every trick but that one."

"Me? That's a laugh!" Gina cried contemptuously.

He exhaled a hissing breath and pivoted from her, violence charging the air around him.

"I am not going to argue with you, Gina," he declared roughly.

"Well, isn't that just fine?" Sarcasm spilled from her lips. "I have a right to be angry. After all, you got us into this mess."

"Your Lady Godiva scene through the streets of town had nothing to do with it, I suppose." His nostrils flared as he cast her a murderous look over his shoulder.

"You were the one who so chivalrously insisted on marrying me," she shot back at him, only to see something flash across his sunbrowned features. That glimpse made her stiffen warily. Very quietly, almost in challenge, she said, "My grandfather said you wanted to marry me."

Arrogance flashed across the angular planes of his face. "Did he?" countered Rhyder in dry mockery.

Gina swallowed, pride keeping her head erect. "Did you want to?" she demanded in a low voice, afraid to hear his answer.

"No." There wasn't a trace of emotion in his

voice. "But that's irrelevant now, since I've made you my wife." He released her from his flat gaze and walked to the telephone. "I'll order your dinner."

A shiver of apprehension raced icily over her flesh. Gina crossed her arms, rubbing her skin to rid it of the foreboding chill, but she only seemed to push it deeper inside. Her knees trembled. She felt weak and frighteningly vulnerable.

Numbly she moved to the bathroom, wishing she had gone there when Rhyder had first suggested it instead of reacting like the child that she kept insisting she wasn't. Gina had learned something that she didn't think she wanted to know. How could the marriage work if they had both been forced into it?

When she returned to the bedroom the question dogged her, nipping and snapping until her nerves were raw. The frayed ends became sensitive to Rhyder's silence. She jumped visibly when a knock at the door announced the arrival of room service and her dinner. Rhyder hadn't ordered anything for himself and Gina had to suffer through swallowing the tasteless food alone.

His jacket and tie had been removed, the cuffs of his white shirt turned back, and the top three buttons unfastened. A brandy he had poured from the portable bar was in his hands as he reclined almost indolently in an armchair. The expression on his hard, tanned features was a study of remoteness.

Gina stared at the food remaining on her

plate. With a jerky movement she let the silverware clatter to the tray and pushed herself away from it, rising in agitation, her fingers twisting into knots. She was conscious of drawing his attention.

"Finished?" Rhyder inquired evenly.

"Yes." Gina flashed him a challenging look.

His mouth thinned into a grim line. "I wasn't going to tell you to clean your plate," he snapped, and downed the swallow of brandy in his glass.

"That's good," she retaliated sharply, "because I wouldn't have done it."

"I was hoping food would improve your disposition." He rose impatiently and walked to the small bar to refill his glass. "But obviously it hasn't."

"So what are you going to do? Drown your sorrow in drink?" Gina taunted.

Bleak blue eyes held the stormy agitation of her ocean green ones, then cut them free as he took a healthy swig from the glass, not savoring the brandy in sips as it was meant to be drunk. The glass was refilled before he moved away from the bar.

"Maybe I've decided that you were right earlier," Rhyder commented with a sardonic lift of an eyebrow. "This might be the night for getting drunk."

Her pulse throbbed unevenly as he lazily approached her. Minus the jacket and tie of civilized dress, and with the opened front of his white shirt revealing the leanly muscled chest, he appeared more like the man her heart remembered, virile and strong with an impression of the sea about him and a rolling deck beneath his feet. Pain splintered through her nerves.

"I'll join you," she declared in a constricted voice.

She started to walk past him to the bar, but his hand shot out to halt her, his fingers closing around the soft flesh of her upper arm. Sore nerves screamed at his firm grip. A thread snapped inside.

"Don't touch me!" she hissed venomously.

"Don't touch you?" repeated Rhyder with sarcastic scorn, tightening his hold. "That's how this whole situation came about, because you begged me to touch you and I refused."

Scorching waves of shame seared through her veins, bringing high color to her face and neck. Futilely she struggled to twist free of his grip, but his fingers dug bruisingly to the bone. She clawed at his hand, trying to make him ease the agonizing pressure.

"Let me go!" It was a desperate cry for mercy because she lacked the strength to make him obey.

Low, harsh laughter came from his throat. "That's not what you wanted me to do before," he mocked her.

Gina made a backhanded swing at his chin, missed, and knocked the brandy glass from his other hand. It fell harmlessly to the thickly carpeted floor, liquid splashing out in a wet stain.

His free hand imprisoned her other arm to

yank her against him. The hint of cruelty in his eyes frightened her and she struggled wildly.

"Let me go! I can't stand you!" she declared, breathing heavily with her efforts.

An iron band crushed her to his chest while hard fingers roughly seized her chin and lifted it upward. "But we're married now, my love," he jeered. "It's all perfectly legal. In fact, it's my conjugal right."

His savage gaze glittered briefly in satisfaction at her fear-rounded eyes before he violently assaulted her quivering lips. He stole the breath from her lungs and drained the strength from her limbs, leaving her limp in his arms. His thirst for revenge wasn't satisfied by simple surrender as he ravaged the sweetness of her mouth, intoxicating brandy on his breath.

Her trembling response to his marauding kiss made little impression on Rhyder. Not until her fingers were curling weakly into his shirt did he ease the pressure of his mouth to masterful possession. His male attraction was something she couldn't fight, nor the wild rapture his lovemaking aroused.

Desire flamed as he plundered the softness of her throat. Her hands inexpertly unfastened the buttons of his shirt so her fingers could glide freely over his hard flesh, smooth as leather.

A gasp of heady pleasure caught in her throat at the touch of his hand sliding open the zipper of her dress. As it fell around her feet, Rhyder lifted her out of it and into his arms. Luminous green eyes blithely met the darkly glowing fires of blue in his gaze.

Without a word, he carried her to the bed and laid her on the scarlet coverlet. A knee rested on the edge of the bed as he towered above her, something primitive and conquering in his stance.

A pagan shiver fluttered Gina's lashes. In the next second, his shirt was discarded and the muscled brown of his naked torso was bending toward her.

CHAPTER FIVE

THE PARTIALLY MUFFLED SOUND of voices wakened Gina the next morning. The pillow was damp beneath her cheek and she remembered sobbing into it last night.

Rhyder had attempted to comfort her, but it had soon become evident that he intended to ease her pain with the same tactics that had caused it in the first place. Gina had cringed from him, inciting his anger, but he had left her alone with her tears.

Very slowly she lifted her head from the pillow and glanced over her shoulder. A shudder of relief quaked through her at the empty pillow beside hers. Warily she looked around the room, but there was no sign of Rhyder.

Then she heard his voice coming from the terrace outside their suite. She listened, unable to figure out whom he could be talking to—until she heard a familiar voice.

"My God, I can't believe you actually married her!" came Pete's astonished exclamation. "When they told me at the harbor, I thought they were pulling my leg. But you actually did it?"

"I had no choice," Rhyder replied, his low voice tautly on edge.

Gina tensed herself, her muscles protesting as she slipped from beneath the covers. Her clothes were still scattered on the floor. She sidestepped them, wanting to forget how they had come to be there, and hurried to her suitcase on the luggage stand.

"But how? Why?" she heard Pete's puzzled voice ask as she pulled a pair of slacks and a top from the folded clothes.

She was just stepping into the slacks when she heard Rhyder answer, "I believe it's commonly known as blackmail."

"Blackmail?" Pete breathed. "What happened while I was gone?"

With frozen movements, Gina finished dressing. She now strained to hear the voice she had tried to ignore. She had to know what his explanation was for that statement.

"She came to the boat late one evening. It was raining and she was soaked to the skin," Rhyder began his explanation tersely. "I went to get a blanket to wrap her in. When I came back with it, the damned little Lolita had taken off her clothes and was begging me to make love to her!"

"Oh, my God!" Pete interjected. "Did you—"

"I told her to go home and grow up!" Rhyder snapped. "She went out of there, crying through the streets, half-naked. Nearly the whole damned town saw her leave the *Sea Witch*."

Gina felt cheap and degraded. The stark truth

of his words shamed her, but she hated him for telling Pete about her wanton behavior. It was too demeaning.

"What did you do then?" Pete wanted to know, incredulity running through his low voice.

"I decided I'd better tell my side of the story before the uproar got so loud nobody would listen, so I went to her house to talk to her grandfather," Rhyder sighed grimly.

"And he didn't believe you?"

"I think he believed me all right." Rhyder exhaled a savage, mirthless laugh. "The trouble was his granddaughter's reputation had been irreversibly damaged in the eyes of the town, a fact he kept drumming into my head as he kept forcing me to drink his whisky."

"You mean he tried to get you drunk?" Pete chuckled his astonishment.

Gina blanched as she remembered the thud of the whisky bottle on the table at least three times before she had buried her head under the pillow. It had been an underhanded trick by her grandfather, regardless of his honorable motives.

"He nearly succeeded. At first I thought it was some kind of test of manhood I was expected to pass. Then I realized, nearly too late, that he intended to keep me from thinking clearly. Not that it mattered either way when he was through," Rhyder tacked on sardonically.

"If you didn't do anything, how could he blackmail you into marrying her? Gina's a nice kid, but what are you going to do with a child bride?" Pete declared in confusion. "I just can't see you giving in to pressure just because of some small town gossip about you and a girl, Rhyder."

"It depends on the pressure." Cynicism deepened his voice to a rough sound. "I was presented with the choice of marrying Gina or answering charges of molesting a minor and attempted rape."

"Good lord!" Pete breathed in sharply.

And Gina sought the support of the luggage rack as her knees gave way. Yesterday, during the drive, she had thought Rhyder was joking when he said he had married her to save his reputation; but he had been dead serious.

"Drunk or sober, I had no choice," Rhyder continued. "The newspapers would have loved the story, especially considering the investigation going on to see if the political contributions made by my father's firm were legal or not. If I'd fought the charges and won, the publicity would still have been damning for my father."

"I'm afraid you're right," Pete agreed in a reluctant tone.

"Gina's grandfather knew he had me between a rock and a hard place. And he squeezed." The words seemed to be drawn through a jaw clenched in anger.

"Does Gina know? Surely she must suspect. Or do you think she was part of it?"

"What you're really asking is, was it all a conspiracy to snare Gina a wealthy husband?" Gina didn't have to see Rhyder to visualize the coldly mocking smile twisting his mouth. "I have no idea. Gina appears unaware of her grandfather's threats. But she also pretended to be a reluctant bride."

"Pretended? What do you mean by that?" Pete was quick to catch the subtly doubting comment.

Closing her eyes, Gina remembered how easily she had allowed his rough kisses to change her attitude. The bitter regret she already felt toward her surrender was doubled. He had seduced her merely to prove a point, not because he had a marital right. She would make him pay for taking her innocence, she vowed.

"Nothing," Rhyder answered Pete's question. "It isn't important."

Her hatred mounted that he could dismiss it so lightly.

"What are you going to do now?" Pete asked, not pursuing the former topic. "I suppose you'll have to take her home to meet your family. Geez, can you imagine her meeting some of your sister's friends? They'll tear the kid apart! Not to mention the claws that will be out from some of the girls who planned on catching you themselves. Are you going to tell your family the truth? About how you were blackmailed into marrying her?"

"Yes," Rhyder snapped, then paused before adding, "they'd never believe that I could fall in love with a teenager. I would be insulting their intelligence by trying to convince them."

"Your sister would never be able to keep quiet about it," Pete warned. "In a month, Clarise would see that everyone knew. It'll be hard on you and Gina. 'Course, you've got a thick skin; you can take it. But the kid . . . ?"

"Maybe she deserves it," was the impatient reply, and Gina's temperature rose.

"Come on, Rhyder. She's young yet."

"Maybe she'll find married life so miserable that I'll be able to buy my freedom with a divorce settlement," Rhyder growled. "In the meantime I'll have to be careful that she doesn't get pregnant, or I could be saddled with her for the rest of my life, one way or another."

"Divorce is expensive," Pete murmured absently.

"I would have paid not to marry her, but that crafty old man had his eye on the main chance. He kept harping on the damage to her reputation. I'd write out a check now, for any sum she'd care to name, if I thought it would get rid of her," Rhyder declared savagely.

Gina straightened from the luggage rack. Cold rage stiffened her shoulders as she walked toward the sliding glass door that opened to the terrace. At the pressure of her hand it glided open, the sound immediately drawing both men's attention.

"How much?" she demanded before either could speak.

A dull red of embarrassment crept under Pete's fair skin. The forbidding hardness of Rhyder's dark features didn't vary at all at the sight of her, expressing surprise at neither her appearance nor her question.

The steel blue of his eyes inspected her in an

alertly sweeping look. The alabaster paleness of her complexion contrasted sharply with the raven blackness of her hair. The ocean green of her eyes had the tempestuous look of a chilling winter storm.

"You said a moment ago you'd be willing to pay to get rid of me. How much?" Gina repeated her question.

"How much do you want?" Rhyder countered smoothly.

Gina named the first large sum that came to mind. Something flickered across the rugged planes of his face and she realized immediately that he had expected her to ask for more.

When she had vowed a moment ago to make him pay, she hadn't meant it in a monetary sense. It didn't matter that she could have asked for more and received it.

"You surprise me, Gina. I would have thought you would put a higher price on your reputation." Rhyder studied her indolently, resting a sun-browned shoulder against a wrought-iron pole supporting the terrace roof.

He was dressed only in dark blue slacks, the morning sun glistening over the bareness of his chest. Gina found the virile thrust of his vitality abrasive, a too vivid reminder of last night's intimacy.

"My reputation is intact," she retorted. "Marrying you made everything all right. You're getting a discount because of it."

"But a divorce so soon?" Rhyder commented

mockingly. "Isn't that going to raise some eye-brows?"

Gina dismissed the question with cold hau-teur. "Oh, they'll click their tongues at me for a while. And they'll probably say that's what you get for marrying a man from away. But when I spread the story around of what a pig you are, they'll agree that I did the right thing. They won't be surprised, considering the kind of man they already think you are, messing around with a child."

The line of his mouth thinned harshly. "You and your grandfather have everything worked out, don't you?"

"We tried not to overlook anything," she lied.

It would have been useless to insist there had been no premeditated scheme to trap him into marrying her. He wouldn't have believed it. Besides, she didn't care what his opinion was of her or her grandfather. They agreed on one point—a swift end to the marriage.

"You'll have your money the minute the di-vorce papers are signed." Contempt sneered in his promise.

"An annulment would be much less compli-cated," Pete inserted hesitantly.

"Yes, and possibly swifter." His steel gaze narrowed thoughtfully on Gina.

"That settles it, then," she declared.

THE ANNULMENT was obtained after Gina had overcome her grandfather's initial objections with threats of running away if he didn't agree. It hadn't been easy continuing her life in the small community.

Although the adults were forgiving of her impetuous and failed marriage, the boys looked at her with different eyes. They glimpsed experience behind the haunted innocence of her face. Her self-respect became a precious commodity to Gina, to be guarded at every turn.

Her grandfather's pride had been offended by the money Rhyder had given her. Nate Gaynes had deposited it in the bank, refusing to touch a penny of it. Gina, too, had felt it was somehow tainted. The bank's reminders of the account and its accumulating interest had seemed to constantly arrive.

Each time she had seen the envelopes in the mail she had wanted to die. Her grandfather became quiet whenever he saw them. Gina sensed that he felt he had failed her by forcing her into the abortive marriage, and she had tried in subtle ways to make him understand that he hadn't known what kind of a man Rhyder was.

In the year that immediately followed the annulled marriage, her grandfather had grown morose and introspective. The next summer he had died in his sleep. In her grief, Gina had blamed Rhyder and had gladly used the money he had given her.

She had rationalized that he owed it to her for causing her grandfather's death. She had sold the house. That last year had erased many of the happy memories that had once been associated with it.

NINE YEARS LATER with her twenty-sixth birthday just celebrated last month, she was a woman with a career and a future before her. So why, Gina bemoaned silently, did such an unwelcome inhabitant of the past have to reenter her life now? All the violent emotions she had thought were buried were surfacing.

Her skin felt hot to the touch. She walked to the sink of the modern-designed kitchen and turned on the cold water to let it run over the inside of her wrists. The outside door opened and she stiffened at the sound, breathing shallowly.

"Gina!" Justin Trent chided her with a mock sigh. "What are you doing in here? The party is outside."

"It was getting a bit hectic out there." She turned off the cold water tap and made a study of drying her hands. "So I came in here to get my second wind."

"You pick the strangest times to withdraw." He walked to her side, took the towel from her hands and tossed it on the counter before taking both her hands in his. "Here I am wanting to show you off to all my friends and you're hiding inside the house."

"I wasn't hiding." Gina forced a smile, unable to meet the warm glow of his brown eyes.

He carried her left hand to his lips, brushing the tips of her fingers with a kiss. Through the concealing veil of her lashes, she saw the wry twist of his sensual mouth as he gazed at her hand.

"I wish you wouldn't wear that ring. It always

makes me feel as if I'm fooling around with someone's wife," Justin mused.

An uncontrollable shiver raced down her spine. Gina quickly removed her fingers from his light hold and turned away, guiltily covering the gold ring with her other hand.

"I told you—it's my grandmother's ring."

The "something old" that her grandfather had sentimentally presented for the wedding, accompanying it with a wish that her marriage to Rhyder would be as long and as happy as his had been.

"You amaze me, honey. Sometimes you're so coolheaded and liberated, thinking only of your career. Then other times you're deliciously old-fashioned and feminine." His finger traced the curve of her cheek. "When I first met you, I thought you wore that ring to keep guys like me away."

"It works for that, too," Gina smiled.

His light caress made her uncomfortable. It came too soon after the memory of another man's touch. But she couldn't draw away from it; Justin wouldn't understand the rejection when she had been allowing him similar little liberties for the last few months. And Gina didn't want to explain or lie.

"It works—unless you want a guy to get closer, mmm?" suggested Justin as his finger tilted her chin upward.

Her lashes closed as his face moved closer. Beneath the warm possession of his lips, hers were stiff and faintly resistant. She tried to relax under his kiss, but the attempt didn't succeed and Justin lifted his head.

Regret trembled through her, regret that she had ever had the misfortune to meet Rhyder and regret that he had suddenly reappeared after nine years.

"As much as I would like to continue in this happy vein—" his mouth hovered near her temple, his moist breath stirring the short black waves of her hair "—I think we'd better return to the clambake, since I'm the host."

"Yes, we should," Gina agreed quickly, anxious to bring an end to the embrace, especially when she was reacting so unnaturally to it.

"You don't need to sound so eager," Justin laughed, and curved an arm possessively around her shoulders.

"Hunger pangs," she lied brightly, walking at his side to the door.

"We'll cure those." Justin ushered her through and slid his arm back to its former position around her shoulders as he escorted her to the gathering of people.

Amid the crowd was Rhyder, magnetically drawing Gina's gaze against her will. His raw masculinity and rough vitality set him apart from the others. His attraction was powerful. Even while she despised him, Gina felt its strength.

Through the crowd, his gaze drifted, caught Gina's look and stopped. She glanced quickly away, her gaze skittering sightlessly in any direction except where Rhyder stood.

Breathing in deeply, she resolved not to let

Rhyder's presence disturb her. The shock of seeing him again was over. As much as she disliked him, she refused to permit him to spoil her enjoyment of the clambake.

"You returned just in time," Katherine Trent spoke up as her brother approached with Gina under his arm. In an aside, she jested to another couple standing near the canvas-mounded trough, "Trust my brother to turn up when the food is ready!"

"I've never been accused of bad timing," Justin responded good-naturedly to the teasing.

Gina slid a surprised glance at her watch. She had been in the house nearly an hour while her mind had run through the events of nine summers ago.

Justin turned to the guests and called, "Come on, everybody. We're ready for the unveiling!"

This time there were plenty of volunteers to help draw back the steam-enclosing canvas and the burlap cloth beneath it. A delicious aroma rose from the mound of seafood and vegetables, mixing in an exotic blend of scents that filled the air. An appreciative murmur ran through the guests.

"It's been years since I've been to a clambake," someone declared, "but that's an aroma I'll never forget!"

Gina glanced in the direction of the voice, an understanding and agreeing smile curving her lips. Rhyder blocked her view, his eyes on her, alertly blue yet masked. The smile faded as her heart tripped over itself.

She was forced to acknowledge that there were many memories that time couldn't dim. Not all of them concerned moments of anger and hatred; remembered moments of desire could blaze in the mind, too. She paled at the discovery wanting to remember only the bitter dislike and never be vulnerable again to humiliation at Rhyder's hand.

"Dig in!" Katherine invited as the bulk of the food was set on a long table, leaving the lobster on the bottom, bright red-pink against the seaweed bed.

With Justin at her elbow, Gina joined the line of people piling food on their plates. She lost sight of Rhyder in the milling group and hoped the separation would be permanent.

"Take our plates to that table over there," Justin said, pointing, as he handed her his plate. "I'll get our lobster and the drawn butter."

As Gina turned to comply, she saw Rhyder seated at the picnic table Justin had indicated. She hesitated but Justin pushed her forward playfully. Other tables were filling up. She couldn't tell Justin that she didn't want to sit at the same table with Rhyder, and there was no other objection she could make to the choice.

Reluctantly she walked toward it. His blue gaze swept uninterestedly over her as she set the plates on the table on the opposite side from where he was sitting. His attention was directed to the couple seated beside him. In seconds Justin returned, balancing two plates while holding on to a cheesecloth bag of clams.

"I don't know what to eat first," the woman across from Gina declared with a laugh.

"Take a bite of everything," the man who was evidently her husband suggested. "Here," he added, reaching for the small bag of clams between their plates, "I'll shuck you a clam."

"That's wrong, Henry," Justin spoke up as Gina helped him set the lobster plates on the table. "A Maine-iac shucks corn, but he 'shocks' clams!"

A discussion followed of other unusual expressions indigenous to the state. Stories were traded between the couple and Justin of humorous incidents they had heard or experienced themselves. Neither Gina nor Rhyder took part.

Once, when Justin was explaining how a term had originated, she had felt Rhyder's gaze touch her. She couldn't help wondering if he was remembering the time she had instructed Pete on the origins of various phrases.

"What about the expression 'happy as a clam'?" The woman frowned.

"Now that one I don't know," Justin admitted.

"Maybe Gina does," Rhyder stated. "She's from down east."

In the middle of breaking a lobster claw, Gina glanced up, momentarily startled by the sound of her name on his lips. The mocking, faintly satirical light in his eyes said he remembered.

"Do you?" the woman prompted.

"'Happy as a clam' is a shortened version," Gina recovered swiftly to explain. "The whole expression is 'happy as a clam at high tide,' for the obvious reason that no one goes digging for clams at high tide."

The trio laughed appreciatively at the droll humor behind the thought. "Down east?" The man called Henry repeated the phrase Rhyder had used. "I always get confused about that. It has something to do with the wind, I know, but would you mind explaining it again?"

"The prevailing wind along the coast of Maine is from the south west. In the days of the clipper ships and other sailing vessels, a ship that left the Boston harbor for some point in Maine would sail 'downwind' in an easterly direction or 'down east.' It's a bit confusing, but anytime you're travelling up the coast of Maine, you're said to be going 'down east,'" Gina concluded.

"That's fascinating, isn't it?" the woman declared. "I remember when we were in . . . " and the conversation shifted to places they had traveled.

Again Gina didn't take part in the discussion, nor did Rhyder. Several times she felt the discomfiting touch of his gaze. The food began to lodge between her throat and her stomach as her tension heightened, but she kept forcing more down, refusing to let him see that his presence had destroyed her appetite.

Her long silence came to Justin's attention and he leaned near her ear. "You're withdrawing again," he whispered.

Gina shook her head, quickly denying it. "I'm eating."

Justin's face was very near hers. Gina knew she had to turn her head only slightly to invite his kiss, but she was too conscious of Rhyder's watching eyes. The other couple rose from the table to refill their plates.

"You've picked your lobster clean," Justin observed after a few seconds. "I'll get you another."

"No. Really, I—" But her protest was wasted as Justin left the table.

"Does he always wait on you?" Rhyder asked dryly.

"Justin is a considerate host." Avoiding his gaze, Gina picked up a clam and made a project out of shocking it.

"Of course," he said with faint derision. Several seconds ticked away in taut silence, then Rhyder began, "Your grandfather—"

"—is dead," she interrupted harshly.

"I'm sorry."

"No, you're not." The flash of her stormy green eyes challenged him to deny it.

There was an arrogant lift of a dark brow before he conceded. "You may be right. Excuse me." And he rose from the table.

Strangely, Gina didn't feel any relief when he didn't return, but drifted among the other guests, some still eating, some replete and leaning back to chat. Eventually he was one of the first guests to leave, but the ghost of his presence remained to haunt her.

It was late in the evening when the last of the guests left and Justin was free to take her home.

She sat silently in the passenger seat, staring into the night as he drove her to her apartment in the city.

"It was a good party, wasn't it?" he commented finally to break the silence.

"Yes, it was," she agreed absently. "Did Rhyder Owens ask any questions about me?" Immediately after the question was out, Gina could have bitten off her tongue for bringing up his name when she had wanted only to forget.

"No." His brown gaze left the highway to glance at her. "You two know each other, don't you?"

Gina hesitated, then decided on the truth. "I met him a long time ago."

"And?" Justin prompted.

"And nothing." She couldn't tell him the rest, not yet.

"How long ago was it?" he persisted, sensing there was more to be told.

"Nine years," she answered shortly.

"You were what? Sixteen?" Gina nodded curtly to the question when Justin glanced at her. "If you remember him after that length of time, he must have been more than a stranger in the crowd. Is he an old flame?"

"Hardly," she denied.

"After nine years, what do you think of him now?"

"That he's still arrogant and self-centered. Let's talk about something more pleasant," she suggested.

Justin complied, a satisfied half-smile curving

his mouth. He talked about the clambake in generalities for the rest of the ride, not once referring to Rhyder in even the most casual way. In front of her apartment he stopped the car, switching off the motor, and turned in his seat.

"Now that we've gotten the small talk out of the way, let's discuss the moon and the stars and—" he reached out to draw her gently toward him "—the beautiful woman in my arms."

With inner reluctance, Gina allowed herself to be curved against his side. "But there isn't any moon," she pointed out.

"We'll pretend," Justin murmured as he lowered his head toward hers.

His kiss was both commanding and tender. Gina's reponse was falsely ardent. The strong circle of his arms did not generate the warm feeling it usually aroused. She blamed herself for his failure to kindle her desire.

The mental barrier was being erected again to make her indifferent to a man's caress. It was a defense mechanism to protect her inner core of passion.

When the embrace reached the stage where it had to grow or die, Gina ended it. His arms tightened in protest to her withdrawal, but she pressed her hands firmly against his chest, wedging a distance between them. Sighing grimly, Justin released her and she smiled an apology.

"Unless you've changed the time of our nine o'clock meeting in the morning," she said gently, "I'm going to have to be up early in order to get to my office and look over the proposals again before meeting you. Which means I need some sleep tonight."

"I don't suppose you're going to invite me in for coffee, are you?" He eyed her ruefully.

"No," she refused with a wide smile.

"Why?" Although lightly asked, the question wanted a serious answer.

"Because if I asked you in for coffee, you would interpret the invitation to mean something entirely different and accept without coffee in mind."

Justin laughed softly at the accuracy of her observation, then studied her quietly for a second. "Are you just playing hard to get with me?"

"I am hard to get." The line of her mouth curved into a smile to take the edge off her words.

"Somebody must have hurt you very badly once." His brown eyes darkened curiously at her startled glance. "I guessed it some months ago. Which probably explains why I've been more patient with you than it's my nature to be. Don't worry," he added as a closed expression stole over her features, "I won't ask you to tell me about him as long as you don't question me about the women I've known before you."

"That's a deal." Gina leaned over and lightly brushed a kiss on his lips. "Good night, Justin. And thank you." There was a magnitude of meaning in the last.

CHAPTER SIX

THE THREE-PIECE BLACK SUIT, consisting of a skirt, waistcoat and jacket, was very masculine in its design, but the ruffled jabot of her white blouse was distinctly feminine. The overall effect was crisply professional while it pointed out the raven sheen of her hair and the contrasting ocean green of her eyes.

With a smooth leather briefcase in her hand, Gina breezed into Justin's outer office. His secretary glanced up from her typewriter and smiled a greeting.

"Mr. Trent is expecting you. You may go right in, Miss Gaynes." The woman nodded toward the inner office door.

"Thank you." Not bothering to knock, Gina opened the door and walked into the plush. executive-designed office.

"Here's my learned attorney now," Justin declared, rising from the chair behind his desk to greet Gina. "She's the secret to my success. Everyone forgets the terms they were negotiating when they deal with her, Mr. Arneson."

The coolly businesslike smile had frozen on Gina's face as she was impaled on the rapier thrust of a pair of steel blue eyes. Seated in a

leather, wing backed chair in front of the massive
walnut desk was Rhyder. A movement near him
finally attracted her stunned gaze.

A third man had been occupying the leather
chair matching Rhyder's. The motion that had
distracted her had been this man rising almost
hypnotically to his feet at the sight of her.

Sandy hair was receding to lengthen his forehead. Dark-rimmed glasses nearly hid his hazel
eyes. The years had matured the features of the
boyish face inclined to freckles, but Gina recognized Pete instantly.

His recognition of her was slower, as if he were
unable to believe it was possible. He glanced at
Rhyder's hardening look for confirmation.

Gina recovered first, walking forward to extend a hand to an astonished Pete. "Hello, Mr.
Arneson."

"It *is* you, Gina," he breathed. Disbelieving
wonder gleamed through the lenses of his glasses
as he held her hand for a long moment without
shaking it. Abruptly his mind registered the for-
mal way she had addressed him, coolly and
politely. "I'm sorry, I . . . I should have said Mrs.
O—"

"Miss Gaynes," she supplied instantly, a
husky tremor of nerves in her voice.

"Oh!" His sandy head jerked slightly. "You
had it legally changed back after—"

"Yes, that's right," Gina interrupted a second
time, and withdrew her hand from Pete's, paling
at the darkening frown on Justin's handsome
face.

"I think I missed something here." Irritation blocked Justin's attempt to make it a laughing declaration.

"It's—" Gina began, but this time she was the one interrupted by Rhyder.

"Gina has unfortunately chosen to keep secret from you, Justin, the fact that she's my wife." Sardonic amusement glittered in the startling blue of his eyes as he met the killing look she threw him.

"Ex-wife," she corrected sharply.

"You were married to him?" Justin's eyes narrowed at Gina. His surprise was equally divided between the fact that she had been married and that Rhyder had been her husband.

Feeling like the accused, Gina stood before the walnut desk, stiffly erect to conceal the inner trembling. Her heart was beating against her ribs like a trapped animal wanting to break free.

Pete was standing to the side, shifting uncomfortably at the situation his astonished words had precipitated. Justin was plainly confused and slightly angered. Only Rhyder seemed to be under his own control as he sat in his chair, relaxed and insouciant.

"I have no idea why Gina changed her name or why she failed to tell you of our marriage," Rhyder said. "Unless, perhaps, she was ashamed of her actions during the brief time we were together."

"I was not!" Gina pivoted to face him, nearly choking on her erupting temper. "I wanted no reminder of our unpleasant association, so I changed back to my maiden name and wiped all trace of you from my life."

"Not quite all," Justin said dryly, his gaze sliding to her wedding band.

Her cheeks crimsoned. "It's my grandmother's wedding ring." But she knew and Rhyder knew that he had been the one to slip it on her finger.

"I wish you'd told me all this yesterday," Justin emitted grudgingly, as if unwilling to admit as much in front of the other two men.

"I had hopes of never seeing him again after yesterday," Gina replied stiffly. "I never expected to walk into your office this morning and see him sitting . . . ." The legal proposals in her briefcase seemed to burn through the leather to scorch her fingers. The turbulent green of her gaze slashed to Rhyder as the significance of his presence registered in her mind. "I presume you are the president of Caufield Enterprises?"

"That's correct," Rhyder nodded with cool mocking arrogance. "Pete is my attorney and he'll be advising me during our negotiations for the resort property that Justin has indicated a willingness to sell."

Her grasp tightened on the briefcase. She turned to Justin with every intention of telling him that he would have to find someone else to represent him. The negotiations would quite likely be lengthy because of the difference between the asking price and the offered price and some complex legal entanglements of the property.

Gina did not want to spend the amount of

time required to arrive at a satisfactory compromise, since the time would be spent in Rhyder's company. But before she could advise Justin of her decision, Rhyder spoke up.

"I think it would be best if we postponed our meeting for a few days, Justin." He rose leisurely to his feet, his gaze glittering briefly on Gina as he stood beside her, towering and masculine, completely in control of his emotions. "I'm certain Gina is as reluctant as I am to sit on opposite sides of a negotiation table. Considering our past association, it will be difficult to be impartial or objective in the discussions needed to reach the various compromises. I quite understand that Gina would prefer that you find another attorney in this matter. Naturally you'll need some time to bring him or her up to date on the various issues."

A raging fire seared through her veins. On the surface it sounded as if Rhyder was offering her an easy way out, but underneath she sensed that he was demanding that she be replaced. His mockery or his sarcasm she could have tolerated, but to be virtually ordered to resign under the guise of thoughtfulness was not something she would accept.

"You are mistaken, Mr. Owens." It sounded ludicrous to call him that, yet it seemed the only way to express the fullness of her anger. "I do not prefer to have Justin hire another attorney. I am much more qualified than anyone else since I am acquainted with you and your methods. I will be better able to protect my client's interest because of it."

Except for the slight darkening of his pupils to a midnight shade, there was no indication from Rhyder that he found her decision objectionable. Yet Gina was certain she had scored a hit. Setting her briefcase on a corner of the desk, she opened it and removed a legal-sized folder.

"I have drafted a land contract agreement to use as a starting point." Gina extracted three copies of the document from the folder and distributed one to each of the men. "It will be more constructive to deal first with the items we agree on."

As he was already familiar with much of the language contained in the proposal, since Gina had discussed it with him in some detail, Justin's perusal of the document was merely a formality. Pete read it with concentration, mentally testing every word and phrase.

With growing irritation, Gina watched Rhyder flip through the multi-page agreement, barely skimming the contents. He didn't even glance at the last page as he tossed it on Justin's desk.

"I find little in it that's agreeable," Rhyder stated flatly.

Counting to ten, Gina held her tongue. If he was attempting to bait her into losing her temper by placing an immediate obstacle in the discussions, she was determined he wouldn't succeed.

"I prefer to hear Pete's opinion," she responded with professional crispness.

There was a condescending, faintly derogatory nod of his jet-dark head. Seething inwardly, Gina ignored the gesture. With negligent ease, Rhyder sat in the chair he had just vacated, relaxing deeply against its winged back.

His hooded gaze made a slow and thorough inspection of her as she waited for Pete to complete his examination of the proposal. Gina pretended to be unaware of Rhyder's eyes on her, but his unwavering gaze was stirring her nerves tautly.

"Excellently drawn," Pete concluded when he had finished reading her proposal. He beamed her a smile that twisted ruefully after a second. "Unfortunately, the language is biased in favor of your client rather than mine. In the points where we are in agreement, I'd like to recommend some changing in the wording."

"Naturally," Gina conceded. Small revisions were to be expected as well as large. She removed a fourth copy from the folder. "Where, specifically?"

As Pete started to turn a page in his copy, Rhyder straightened with undisguised impatience. "Pete and I will look over the proposal, make some notes, and get back to you in the next few days, Justin."

He was already walking toward the door by the time Pete assimilated the information that Rhyder had brought the meeting to an abrupt end. Self-consciously Pete glanced at Gina. The grim set of her lips no longer concealed her anger. Mumbling a goodbye, he picked up his briefcase, the proposal folded in his hand, and followed Rhyder's retreating back.

Silence descended with the closing of the door. Gina stared at it, wondering how she could have been so foolish as not to resign. It had been what she wanted and what Rhyder had wanted. Why had she sailed into the teeth of danger?

A faint movement behind her reminded her of Justin's presence in the room, and the explanations he would want. At the moment, she didn't want to give them.

Briskly she turned to the desk and stuffed her copy of the proposal into the folder to slip it into her briefcase. Justin watched, waiting silently. With a slight toss of her head, Gina looked at him and smiled distantly.

"The meeting didn't end on an auspicious note, but Rhyder wants the property or he wouldn't have come all this way." Her business-like manner deliberately didn't encourage any personal questions. "Give me a call whenever he contacts you."

She turned to leave, but was halted by his low, demanding voice. "Gina."

"Yes, Justin?" She glanced over her shoulder, false curiosity in the arch of an eyebrow.

"Why didn't you tell me you were married to him?" The strong line of his jaw was thrust forward at an aggressive angle.

"It seemed unnecessary."

"Unnecessary?" He was about to say more, but checked himself with an effort. "How much of what you did tell me was true?"

"All of it," Gina replied stiffly.

"Does that means you were married to him nine years ago? When you were sixteen?" Justin tipped his head to one side, skepticism and censor in his expression.

"Yes, which is in itself an explanation," she retorted.

"Yet you denied he was an old flame," he accused.

"He's a dead flame as far as I'm concerned." Their chemistries still mixed with explosive results, but it was due to hostility, not passion.

"Dammit, Gina!" His fist slammed against the desk top in anger. "You could have warned me who he was instead of letting me believe that he was someone you had a summer flirtation with years ago!"

"If I had known he was the president of Caufield Enterprises, I would have told you about him!" Gina flashed. "As it was, you didn't bother to tell me."

"I supposed you knew," Justin defended. "I certainly wasn't trying to keep it a secret from you. You certainly can't say the same."

"I don't appreciate your insinuations!" She unleashed the anger that had been smoldering beneath the surface, kindled by Rhyder. "Nor do I like being cross-examined as if I were on trial for some crime!"

"Can you blame me for feeling as if I've been betrayed?" he demanded.

Breathing in deeply, Gina fought to control

her temper. "If you prefer to have another lawyer represent you, you're free to do so, Justin."

He didn't try to stop her as she walked out of
his office. The legal firm Gina worked for had
offices in a building several blocks from Justin's.
The walk in the brisk autumn air cooled most of
her anger by the time she entered the reception
area.

A telephone message to call Justin was await-
ing her arrival. In the small cubbyhole that was
her office, Gina dialed his number, bracing herself for the clipped announcement that he was
hiring another lawyer. His voice was clipped, but
he told Gina that he still wanted her to represent
him in the negotiations.

Professionally it was a victory, since she had
been slowly building a reputation in real estate
dealings. Yet she knew that emotionally it would
have been better to have lost this one and not
been forced to tolerate Rhyder's company.

TWO DAYS LATER, Gina received a counterproposal in the mail from Pete Arneson on Rhyder's
behalf. She had just finished reading it when her
extension rang. It was Justin calling to tell her
that Rhyder had scheduled a meeting for the
following afternoon.

Gina told him about the counterproposal she
had received. "If Rhyder thought our proposal
was unacceptable, his is ludicrous."

"I don't think there's much doubt that we're
going to have a fight on our hands to get what we

want," Justin replied in a tone that said he wasn't looking forward to it.

"So will Rhyder," she said with a decisive note of battle.

Her opinion of his counterproposal was repeated the next afternoon to Rhyder's face. Immediately Gina ignored him to discuss some of the minor differences with Pete, choosing ones that could quickly be resolved.

Rhyder stepped in and they became embroiled in a bitter dispute on a major issue. After nearly an hour of verbal sword-clashing, Gina tossed her pencil onto the table beside her long yellow note pad.

"These guarantees you're asking Justin to make are preposterous!" she declared in exasperation. "From the beginning, you've been aware of the boundary dispute to the south. You can't expect him to guarantee the outcome of that."

"I can and do." There was uncompromising hardness to the line of his jaw.

A long, slow fuse began to burn. "Can you guarantee that after these negotiations are over you and I will never see each other again?" Gina challenged, meeting the hard steel in his startling blue eyes. "Because if you can, I will advise Justin to agree to yours."

His carved mahogany features darkened. "I didn't think you could keep personalities out of these discussions, Miss Gaynes," he said in a savage undertone.

Gina stiffened, paling at his harsh taunt. The

burning fuse nearly reached the dynamite of her temper before she was able to check it. With controlled movements, she began gathering her papers and replacing them in her briefcase, aware of the silence that had suddenly descended on the room.

The briefcase was shut before she looked at any of them. Then it was Pete who received the blast of her green eyes, as cold as the Atlantic in winter.

"I'm wasting my time here. It's pointless to sit here and argue when I have work to do in my office." Gina rose from her chair. "When your client is willing to be reasonable and compromise some of his impossible demands, we can resume these talks." Her gaze sliced to Justin, who was both amazed and uncertain. "I'll talk to you later."

To Rhyder she said nothing, sweeping out of the room without a glance at him. She paused in the outer office long enough to ask Justin's secretary to telephone her office and let them know she wouldn't be returning that afternoon. Then she walked.

Cold fury drove her for blocks. Finally she ended up, exhausted and footweary, only a block from her apartment. The problem was, her car was parked in the lot near her office building.

Reluctantly she started to retrace her steps. With a sigh she stopped and walked to her apartment. The car was locked and would be relatively safe until tomorrow. She could take a taxi to the office in the morning.

Inside her apartment, her knees began to tremble. A tear slipped from her lashes, trickling down her cheek. It was the first time she could remember crying since her grandfather had died.

The telephone rang. Gina guessed it was Justin or one of her girl friends and let it ring unanswered. As she started to fill the bathtub, its demanding call started again, but she ignored it and added perfumed bath salts to the water.

The telephone continued to ring intermitently during her long soak in the bubble bath. The fragrant water soothed her tired muscles and strained nerves.

Wrapped in a short cotton robe, she walked into the kitchen and poured a glass of milk from the refrigerator. When she stepped into the living room, the telephone started ringing again. Gina stopped, frowning at the beige telephone and the persistence of her caller.

On the sixth ring she answered it, impatient with herself for giving in to its demands, yet knowing her caller appeared determined not to give her any peace until she did.

"This is Rhyder," the masculine voice unnecessarily identified itself.

Her first impulse was to slam the receiver on its cradle, but she checked herself and asked curtly, "What do you want?"

"If you're over your tantrum and have stopped sulking, I would like to arrange a meeting for this evening," he taunted dryly.

"I'm a lawyer, not a doctor. I'm not on call at all hours of the day and night," Gina snapped.

"If it's a meeeting you want, call Justin and arrange it for tommorrow."

"There is other property I can buy, not quite as ideally located as Justin's, but with the potential for development and minus the hassle I'm getting from you. You either agree to this meeting tonight or the deal is off," Rhyder promised with ominous calm.

"Don't threaten me, Rhyder!" she breathed angrily.

"But I am. And considering that you were the one to walk out on today's meeting after issuing your ultimatum, you'll have a difficult time convincing Justin that you're acting in his best interests by refusing to meet me tonight," he suggested complacently. "Justin stands to make a sizable profit from this sale. He isn't going to like losing it, nor thank you for causing it."

"And of course you'll make sure he knows that you were willing to make concessions on some of your demands if only I'd met you halfway." Sarcasm honed a sharp edge to her voice. "You'll tell him that even if it's a lie."

"But neither of you would ever be certain it was, would you?" countered Rhyder.

"What time?" Gina surrendered reluctantly.

"Seven-thirty."

She glanced at her wrist, but it was bare. "What time is it now?"

"A few minutes before six," he answered.

There was plenty of time to eat a cold meal, dress and travel downtown. "Seven-thirty at Justin's office," Gina said confirming the hour and location.

"Since it's after business hours, I thought we'd meet at the apartment I've rented." Rhyder paused. "Unless, of course, you object to meeting here?"

Part of her objected strongly. However, to admit that would also mean admitting she was allowing personalities to enter a business negotiation, the very thing Rhyder had accused her of today. She wasn't going to give him a second opportunity.

"Why should I?" Gina returned with false unconcern. "What's the address?"

She set her glass of milk on the telephone stand and reached for the pencil and message pad beside the phone, writing down the address as Rhyder gave it to her. When he had hung up she tore the top paper from the pad and fingered it apprehensively.

An inner sense warned her that she was making a mistake, but it was too late for second thoughts. She had committed herself and now had to follow through.

Returning to the kitchen with her glass of milk, she made a quick salad of cold shrimps from the refrigerator, ate half of it before her appetite waned, and stacked the dirty dishes in the sink.

Nothing in her closet appealed to her as she tried to choose what to wear. Slacks seemed too casual without a jacket, and the evening was warm. Finally she decided on a slightly flared white skirt and a scarlet tunic with a matching overblouse patterned with scarlet and pink flowers.

She regretted her choice when the cab driver knocked at her apartment door and pursed his lips in a silent whistle of admiration at the sight of her, but there wasn't time to change. The briefcase was in her hand as Gina locked her apartment door and followed the driver to his cab. It was almost a shield against her femininity, a gossamer one, more to protect her from herself.

The cab driver kept up a steady flow of chatter all the way to Rhyder's apartment building. She wished for silence to consider her legal strategy for the approaching meeting with Rhyder, but her monosyllabic responses didn't discourage him. Usually she was able to block out unwanted sounds, but this time she wasn't able to concentrate.

CHAPTER SEVEN

THE DRIVE DIDN'T TAKE as long as Gina had expected. At twenty minutes past seven she knocked on Rhyder's door. When it opened, her senses leaped, reacting to the vibrantly male figure standing before her.

The vivid green pattern of his silk shirt made Rhyder's eyes appear even more blue. Darker green trousers were tailored to loosely mold his hips and muscular thighs.

"The others haven't arrived yet, have they?" There was a nervous catch to her voice as she tried to sound professional and poised.

"No." He opened the door wide. "Come in." His gaze raked her length, a remoteness in his look. Motioning toward the living room behind him, he said, "Make yourself comfortable."

Impossible, Gina thought as she acknowledged his invitation with a stiff smile. The room was decorated in complementing beige and peach tones with a russet shade for contrast. Highly impractical but definitely luxurious, she decided. She wondered about the view from the window, but the drapes were closed against the western sun.

"I'm having a drink. Would you like one?" Rhyder inquired with distant politeness.

"A glass of white wine if you have it," Gina accepted, sitting down on a plush beige sofa and placing her briefcase on the adjoining sofa cushion.

The palms of her hands were damp with nervous perspiration. She wished Pete or Justin would arrive. The apartment walls seemed to echo the knowledge that she was alone with Rhyder. An office meeting would have been infinitely preferable to this informal situation. It brought the business relationship to a more casual level.

Her nerves tensed as Rhyder approached. He didn't hand her the wine goblet, but set it on the end table nearest her instead. Gina was aware that by doing so he had avoided accidentally touching her.

When he sat down in an armchair near the sofa, she knew she was incapable of small talk, especially when she noticed the brandy glass he held in his hands. Instantly her mind flashed back to the night of their wedding. She turned to the briefcase beside her and snapped it open.

"We might as well start—"

"Save it for later." His low voice cut across her sentence, faintly harsh but controlled.

Gina hesitated for a split second, then closed the case. Reaching for her wineglass, she leaned against the sofa back, trying to appear relaxed. There was a slight tremor in her hand as it carried the glass to her lips. She sipped the dry

Chablis quickly and held the glass in both hands.
Her nerves vibrated under the watchfulness of
Rhyder's gaze.

"I've heard some glowing reports about you
from your fellow members of the bar. You seem
to have made remarkable progress in the short
time since you passed your exams." He absently
swirled the brandy in his glass, his compelling
eyes not leaving her.

"Thank you. I've been fortunate." She didn't
want him to compliment her, if that was what he
was doing.

"The fact that you're beautiful brought you
more quickly to the attention of the male members of your profession, no doubt, and aided the
swift recognition that you were intelligent, as
well." There was a hint of cynicism in the twisting mouth. Before Gina could decide if he was
being offensive, Rhyder continued, shifting his
attention to the amber brown liquid in his glass.
"With your background, I would have thought
you'd follow in your father's footsteps, specializing in marine law instead of real estate and land
contracts."

"I seemed to have a natural aptitude for this
field and chose it," was her only explanation.

Rhyder drank a swallow of brandy and gave
her a considering look. "You mentioned at the
clambake that your grandfather was dead. Has it
been long?"

His bland questions expressed a polite interest
in her, yet Gina felt agitated by them. Courtesy
demanded that she answer them. She had to

either keep up her part in this tension-charged truce or begin the quarrel that would destroy it.

"Eight years." Giving in to the restless stirrings caused by unwelcome memories, she rose from the sofa and wandered to the fireplace, a combination of rust- and sand-colored stone.

Rhyder didn't make any gesture of sympathy, probably remembering her rejection of his previous attempt at the clambake. "What did you do afterward?"

"I sold the house and went to college." It was several seconds before Gina realized she had condensed eight years of living into a few short sentences.

Drinking the last of her wine, she held on to the empty glass. It gave her hands something to do. She glanced covertly at her wristwatch, wondering when Justin and Pete would arrive. Soon, she hoped. The atmosphere was beginning to be stilted.

"More wine?" Rhyder offered, rising from the armchair to walk to the bar to refill his own glass.

"No, thank you," she refused.

"How long have you known Justin?" Something in the cobalt darkness of his look across the room made Gina uneasy. The question did not sound as politely indifferent as the others. Warily she hesitated.

"I met him shortly after I came to Portland to work for my present firm," she answered finally. "I've represented Justin in several land transactions similar to this one."

His mouth twisted cynically as he lifted the

brandy glass to within inches of it. "Do you mean it's a business relationship you have with him?" he asked over the rim of his glass.

Her tongue quivered with the urge to tell him it was none of his business, but if she held her temper a little longer, Justin or Pete would come and the conversation would leave these personal topics.

"I do see Justin socially," she admitted. Rhyder had to have known that. Justin had made it fairly obvious at the clambake.

"Often?" He moved leisurely to where she stood in front of the fireplace.

Her chin lifted to a defiant angle, letting him know he had no right to question her, but she answered him anyway, coolly, concealing her anger.

"I suppose several times a week could be considered often."

He held her gaze. "Do you sleep with him?"

The tight rein on her temper snapped. It unleashed her hand in a swinging arc, her opened palm stinging numbly against his hard cheek. When her green eyes focused on the slowly reddening white mark near his jawline, she realized what she had done. She took a quick step backward, expecting the swift retaliation she remembered so well.

Rhyder didn't move. He was a statue, carved in hardwood, not blinking an eye, yet intimidating Gina until her heart raced in panic.

"Does that mean yes or no?" he asked levelly.

"That means it's none of your business!" she retorted, breathing rapidly.

"It is my business." Rhyder drained the brandy glass and set it on the mantelpiece. ":Don't forget, Gina, that I know you, too, and your methods."

More than ever before, Gina didn't trust him. "What's that supposed to mean?" she asked guardedly.

"It means I'm wondering how far you'll go in forcing me to agree to Justin's terms," Rhyder explained, his expression hardening in contempt.

"Forcing you?" Bewilderedly Gina shook her dark head, caution in her frown. "The terms are to be negotiated."

"Will blackmail be part of the negotiations?" His sardonic query chilled her to the bone.

"Blackmail?" The word was repeated unknowingly.

"Don't pretend you haven't heard of the word," he mocked her savagely. "You've used it before." Gina paled. "But it can be dangerous," Rhyder continued. "I don't think you'd risk it unless you were deeply involved with Justin."

"Blackmail?" Gina repeated, angrily this time. "How on earth could I blackmail you?"

"That innocent act won't work, Gina," he jeered. "You were hoping I wouldn't know, but unfortunately I do."

"Know what? You're talking in circles!" But Gina felt she was the one caught in the maelstrom.

"You're a lawyer." Rhyder towered above

her, dark and cynical, his powerful maleness a threatening thing. "You know as well as I do that our annulment isn't worth the paper it's printed on."

His harsh statement hit her with the force of a body blow. "What?" she gasped.

"That was perjured testimony I gave under oath," he said coldly. "Technically it invalidates the annulment. Which means, Gina, that you are still my wife."

"No," Gina protested widly. "It can't be true! How? Why?"

His gaze narrowed to piercing steel, slicing over her white face. "To put it delicately, I swore that our marriage was never consummated."

Gina pivoted from him, her fist clenched against her stomach. "Why? Why did you do it?"

"It was the quickest way to end our marriage," Rhyder snapped. "And the cheapest. Divorce can be too complicated and prolonged. You were willing to accept a relatively small settlement and I didn't want to take the chance you would change your mind and ask for more or decide not to end the marriage at all. It wasn't until later that I learned how precarious the separation was."

She closed her eyes, trying to pretend it was all a bad dream if only she could wake up. A vise was clamped on her forearm. The brutal pressure jerked her to face him, snapping her eyes open to be subjected to the harsh glitter of his.

"Are you trying to convince me that you didn't

know this?" Rhyder twisted Gina's arm in front of him to draw her nearer.

"I didn't know," she insisted, caught between confusion, anger and fear. "I didn't think." Realization dawned on the reason behind his question. Indignation surfaced. "You believed I intended to blackmail you with the fact that our marriage might possibly be invalid because of your testimony, didn't you?"

"I expected it, yes," he admitted without a trace of apology in his condemning tone. "You weren't above blackmailng for money once. Why shouldn't you do it again?"

"Because—" violence stormed within, emotions whipped and churning from a blacklash of guilt and flaring at his unwarranted accusation "—all I wanted was to eliminate you from my life. I took your money because it's the only thing men like you value and I wanted to make you pay for what you had done to my grandfather and me! I wanted you gone!"

Shooting fire flamed from her imprisoned arm as Rhyder increased the pressure of his grip. Her fragile bones threatened to snap under his crushing hold. Gina reacted instinctively, fighting and straining against the steel trap of his fingers, suffering the madness of a wild animal that would destroy itself rather than submit to capture.

Holding her easily, Rhyder tightened his grip fractionally. Pain weakened her legs, allowing him to pull her closer. The ruthless set of his jaw was menacingly grim with purpose. Fear ran unchecked as Gina struggled in wild desperation.

"So you wanted to eliminate any trace of me from your life?" he mocked her cruelly. His other hand closed around her throat, digging into the tender flesh beneath her jaw. "Wipe away this if you can."

The force of his hand stretched her neck as he lifted her face to receive the descending fury of his mouth. Her free arm came up to rigidly brace her hand against a muscled shoulder, holding him away.

But her lips were brutalized by his savage possession. She strained away to avoid the punishment and degradation he intended to inflict. To a small degree she succeeded, not allowing him to crush her stiff lips.

"I despise you for this." She choked out the words his mouth tried to smother.

It angered Rhyder that she was capable of any resistance. Gina felt it in the rippling muscles of his shoulder. His strangling fingers left her throat and shifted their biting grip to the back of her neck.

The stiffened arm that had kept him at arm's length from her gave way under his renewed assault. Overpowered by his brute strength, she was jerked against him.

The sudden contact with the rock wall of his chest knocked the breath from her lungs. His mouth smothered hers, not allowing Gina to regain it. Blackness swirled behind her closed eyes, weakening her resistance.

His shoulders seemed to wrap around her, dwarfing her with their breadth. She couldn't stop the hands that molded her curves to fit the hard contours of his male length.

Something melted—not in Gina but in Rhyder. The feel of her soft flesh pressed against him stole his wrath. He was no longer ruled by vengeance. The hardness of the arms around her and the bruising pressure of the mouth claiming hers didn't lessen, but subtly changed to exert mastery rather than punishment.

A clock inside her head started to turn backward. The years began to roll away until she was carried back in time. Embers of desire that she had believed were dead ashes were rekindling. Their glowing heat spread through her veins, her heart throbbing with a song she had thought forgotten.

Sensual longings flamed under the expert persuasion of Rhyder's mouth. In moments she would be lost, completely under his control. It would be the final humiliation. Gathering the last remnants of her pride, she wrenched free of his arms, nearly stumbling in the shaky steps she took to put distance between them.

Hugging her arms around her waist, she tried to assuage the empty ache in the pit of her stomach. Her back was to him. She couldn't risk looking at him; the rough carving of his dark features was too rawly virile and handsome. A tremor of vulnerability shivered down her spine as she sensed him moving toward her. She had to deny the way he aroused her.

"The only thing I want from you is to get out of my life and stay out. It's all I've ever wanted!" she declared hoarsely when Rhyder stopped behind her.

For nine years Gina had convinced herself that she hated him. But if he touched her now, her heart would overrule her mind just as it had before. Closing her eyes tightly, she prayed he wouldn't, her nerves tensing under the regard of his eyes.

Something brushed the tapering shortness of her dark hair near the back of her neck. Gina flinched, taking a quick step forward to elude his fingertips. Her heart fluttered wildly as she swallowed the soft moan in a faint sigh.

"When did you cut your hair?" Rhyder's musing voice inquired—distant yet warm. An underlying hardness in its tone kept it from suggesting a caress.

"Some time ago." She tried to sound indifferent, but she couldn't match his remoteness.

"Why?" He persisted in the subject, ignoring her previous disclaimer that she wanted him out of her life.

And Gina couldn't find the words to remind him of it. He was standing too close for her to think clearly. An inner radar was conscious of the scant distance that separated them.

"It was impractical," she answered nervously. "Besides, long hair went out of style."

"It never goes out of style," Rhyder corrected her with dry mockery. The inflection of his voice changed as he commented absently, "Your hair always reminded me of midnight satin. Sleek and shiny with blue-black lights."

A compliment from him was more than the disturbed state of her nerves could handle. There was no protection in not facing him, so Gina turned around. His electric blue gaze jolted through her, charged with the high voltage of his physical attraction.

For a numbed moment, she could only stare at him. His ebony hair grew with wayward thickness, falling carelessly across his tanned forehead. Dark brows almost levelly curved above the deeply brilliant blue of his eyes. Slanting away from the faintly patrician bridge of his nose was the chiseled prominence of his cheekbones. The aggressive thrust of his jaw and chin accented the cynical lines carved on either side of his hard, sensual mouth.

Over it all was a mahogany mask to conceal his thoughts. Vitally male, his strength, power and determination were etched in his features for anyone to see. Gina was shaken by the discovery that he would allow nothing to stand in his way. She recoiled from the ruthlessness she knew was there.

"Why did you have to come to Maine? Why couldn't you have bought property someplace else?" Gina protested in angry despair. "I don't want you here! All I want to do is forget!" She could have if he hadn't come back. "Why couldn't you stay away? Why couldn't you forget about me?"

The mask was discarded and seething rage

tempered his gaze with the fine edge of cutting steel. It sliced over Gina's face, pinning her on its sharp point and refusing to let her turn away.

"That's what you were hoping, wasn't it?" Rhyder accused. "When I met you at the clambake, you were hoping I wouldn't recognize you." His nostrils flared in contempt as Gina shook her head mutely, unable but wanting to deny he spoke the truth. "Don't bother to lie," he hissed. "I saw it in your eyes that day." A fury seemed to build within him as soon as he said that. "Damn those eyes!" It exploded from him as he spun to the side.

At the last moment he had controlled the violence of his emotion, and Gina shuddered, not understanding what had caused it and only guessing she was somehow to blame. Her legs felt weak beneath her. "Those eyes of yours have haunted me from the first time I saw you," Rhyder began to explain, his voice vibrating huskily with the tautness of his control. "Green as the ocean. Dangerous, uncharted, and as enthralling as the sea. Do you think I didn't try to forget you?" His gaze slashed to her, cutting her to ribbons.

Yet a part of her thrilled to the negative implication of his question. Rhyder had found her as impossible to forget as she had found him. But it seemed unlikely that it could be true when he had been so eager to get rid of her nine years ago.

"I don't believe you." Gina blinked her widened eyes, trying to armor herself with pride.

He studied her in silence. "My boat could have been named after you," he said with cynical bitterness. "The *Sea Witch*. That's what you were and that's what you are. You're some kind of a witch that drives a man mad. That spell you cast was potent. Nine years, and it still has the power to dull my reasoning."

"I don't know what you're talking about," she murmured, chilled by the icy loathing in his voice.

"Don't you?" Rhyder jeered. "For the last nine years, every time I saw the ocean, it was the liquid green of your eyes before me. Night darkness was the black of your hair. Sunlight, the pale golden shade of your skin. Its warmth like when you touched me."

"No, it can't be true," Gina protested in a helpless whisper.

He continued as though he hadn't heard her. "I heard about this property for sale. It was ideal for the diversification we'd planned, but I found myself rejecting it because it was in Maine and that's where you were. I didn't come to find you or persecute you. I came to put your ghost to rest. Within hours of my arrival, who is the first person I see?"

Gina swallowed. His anger was closer to the surface again, transmitting its changed vibrations to her already raw and sensitive nerve ends. She felt defensive and knew she had no reason to be.

"I was just as stunned to see you," she insisted stiffly

"Were you? It didn't show." The gibe rolled caustically from his thinning lips. "You greeted me very calmly with another man's arm around your waist, denying that you ever knew me and informing me that your name was Miss Gina Gaynes. Do you know what my first reaction was?"

"No." Gina shook her head briefly, wanting to stop the acid flow of explanation that was burning her ears.

"That you were trying to conceal from Justin the fact that you'd been married before. I felt sorry for him until you walked into the office the next morning. When I realized you were a lawyer, I knew I was the one being set up again. You thought I was an easy target, didn't you?" challenged Rhyder.

"That isn't true." She averted her gaze, running a hand through the short hair near her ear. "I tried not to think about you at all."

"Were you hoping I'd married again? That would have been perfect for your scheme, wouldn't it? Then you could have confronted me with bigamy charges."

"I didn't hope you were married." Strangely, Gina had never pictured him marrying another woman during the nine years. The thought now churned her stomach. "I didn't want to know about you or your life after . . . ." She couldn't finish that. "And I told you I didn't know about the annulment. I never had any intentions to threaten you with anything, I swear!"

Rhyder laughed harshly in disbelief. Gina felt

herself bridling at his continued failure to accept her word. It was his testimony that had voided the annulment.

"When you found out we were still legally married, you should have contacted me," she accused, taking the offensive. "I would have gladly given you a divorce."

"For how much?" he flashed savagely.

"Money! It always comes down to money with you, doesn't it?" Gina stormed.

"You started it." Rhyder towered before her, his hands on his hips as he glared coldly. "You were the one to put a price tag on the annulment. It was your suggestion, not mine."

"No, it wasn't," she denied coolly, secure in the truth of what she was saying. "You were the one who mentioned it first."

"That's a lie!"

Gina lifted her chin, meeting the blue contempt of his gaze. "I heard you on the terrace talking to Pete the morning after we were married. You said you would have paid anything not to marry me." The humiliating words were branded into her memory. "And you would write a check for any amount to get rid of me. After all the other degrading things you said to Pete, do you honestly think I would have wanted to stay married to you?" she demanded bitterly.

"You didn't hate me so much that you wouldn't take my money," he reminded her arrogantly.

"Yes, I took it," Gina admitted, breathing with difficulty. "You couldn't understand anything that wasn't measured by money. But it never restored my grandfather's honor because my behavior had shamed him. And he thought he'd failed me. That's why he died, because of you. He wanted me to be married and happy, as happy as he was with my grandmother." Anguish was strangling her voice. "How could I be happy with you when you kept calling me a teenager and a child bride?" For an instant she had the strength to run, but his hands reached out, catching her by the hips and forcing her to remain in place. She tried to push them away, but he held her firmly.

"For God's sake, how do you think I felt?" he demanded angrily. "You were only sixteen! I was an adult, supposedly possessing a certain amount of decency. Do you know how disgusting it was to discover I hadn't the self-control to keep my hands off an innocent, if bewitching, young girl? You chased me—you know that. It was almost a game with you. You invited me to kiss you, to make love to you, while only half knowing what it was about."

Her cheeks crimsoned at his words, in shameful awareness of the truth. His hands burned into her hips, reminding her that even now his touch could enflame her with desire.

"But you weren't the first young girl to pursue me, Gina." As if he read her thoughts, his hands tightened on her hips, drawing her fractionally closer to him. "The others I ignored very easily. With you, it was impossible. I kept reminding myself that I was the adult, the one who had the sense to not let things get out of hand. But I didn't. When I was with you, I never felt any decency or consideration for your tender age, only lust.''

His hands slid to her waist, holding her for a second while her pulse raced at the darkening light in his eyes. She was a willing prisoner of his touch, pliantly allowing herself to be drawn against him. The hardness of his muscular length supported her as she leaned on him.

Her dark head was tipped back to gaze at his face. The warmth of his breath fanned her cheeks. Beneath her hand, resting on his chest, she could feel the drumbeat of his heart, in tempo with her own.

"The only thing that's changed in nine years—'' Rhyder spoke slowly, his eyes shifting their attention to her lips ''—is that now you're a woman. Everything else is the same. You'd think after all this time I would find that I wouldn't want to make love to you. But I do.''

"Rhyder, no—''

He covered her lips with his open ones. They parted of their own volition, inviting the mind-shattering exploration of his mouth. He devoured their sweetness for spellbinding minutes, then moved with tingling ease to the sensitive lobe of her ear.

"Please, don't do this,'' Gina murmured. Lacking the will power to resist and knowing she would hate herself for being weak, she pleaded with him in hopes that he would have the decency to stop.

"You know you want me to," he answered complacently, certain now of the power he had over her.

"Pete, Justin, they could come any minute," she protested as she fought through the waves of sensual pleasure for some lifeline to keep her from drowning.

"No, they won't." Rhyder brought his lips to the corner of her mouth. "The only meeting I had planned was between you and me."

CHAPTER EIGHT

GINA TWISTED SLIGHTLY to elude the fire of his lips, her mind already dizzy from their warmth. "But you said—" she murmured bewilderedly.

"—that I wanted to arrange a meeting for tonight. I made no mention of anyone attending it except you and me," Rhyder finished.

His caressing fingers slipped the impeding collar of her flowered overblouse aside as he sought the base of the sensitive cord at the crook of her neck. His light nibbling sent quivers through her flesh.

"That isn't fair," she protested, although primitive yearnings made her voice breathless with surrender.

She was molded to the male contours of his length. It was impossible for her to be unaware of his need for her, and it intensified the throbbing ache she felt. Rhyder caught her chin and lifted it to gaze deeply into her eyes.

"What is fair, Gina?" he demanded, his low voice raw with desire, its unspoken message quaking through her. "Was it fair for you to haunt me for nine years? Has it been fair these last few days to see you and never have the chance to touch you to find out if the fire in my soul was for a ghost or a woman?''

His features were set in uncompromising lines. There would be no turning back for Rhyder. Gina saw this as her heart swelled to the rough handsomeness of his face, so very strong and so very male.

"You tricked me," her mind forced her to murmur as it continued its war with her emotions.

The cobalt blue of his eyes, smoldering and compelling, held her gaze effortlessly while his hands slipped from her chin to join his other hand in sliding the overblouse from her shoulders to fall to the floor at her feet. Rhythmically he stroked her bare arms in an arousing manner.

"Yes, I tricked you," he agreed. Exploring fingers left her arm to find the neckline zipper of her tunic. A thumb trailed along her spine as he unzipped it. The sensous caress played havoc with her senses. "I had to see you tonight. I couldn't wait any longer. If you hadn't come, I would have been at your apartment, battering down the door. You hated me nine years ago for taking your innocence and you've damned me for your grandfather's death. What difference does it make now if I add another item to the list of reasons to hate me?"

His hands slipped beneath the material of her tunic and began sliding it up. Gina struggled weakly to interfere with his movements, but his touch was scalding against her bare skin.

"No!" she protested even as he succeeded.

Rhyder drew her onto her tiptoes, burying his mouth in the exposed hollow of her throat. A hand was tantalizingly near the lacy cup of her brassiere. White heat raced madly through her veins.

"You cast too potent a spell, Sea Witch." As he bent her backward, the moistness of his mouth followed the curve of her breastbone.

But it was his magic that was enthralling Gina. Her arms were gliding to his neck to curl her fingers in the ebony blackness of his hair.

It was with surprise that she heard herself say, "This isn't right."

Rhyder swung her off her feet and into his arms. "You are my wife, Gina," he stated huskily, looking down at her. "You belong to me."

In her heart she knew he was right and let her lips tell him so when his dark head bent to claim them. His strength became a thing to glory in and not fight, even in token resistance.

Later, when the heady rapture was receding under a cold wave of reality, Gina shivered and would have slid away. Rhyder's arm reached out to curve around the nakedness of her slender waist and draw her back to the warming heat of his body.

"This time there aren't going to be any tears, Gina," he told her as he gently shaped her to his side, her head resting on his muscled shoulder.

A SENSATION OF COOLNESS awakened Gina the next morning. She turned to find Rhyder and nestle against his warmth, but he wasn't there.

The inner radiance glowing in her eyes was dimmed by the discovery. She sat up, unable to shake the nightmarish feeling of dread that this had happened before.

Her clothes were neatly folded and laid across a chair back. Certainly they were not where they had been left. She slipped from beneath the covers to dress with hurried motion. As she started to slip the scarlet tunic over head, she heard the sound of voices in another part of the apartment. For a moment, she was paralyzed by the chilling sensation of déjà vu.

Almost against her will, Gina was driven to the bedroom door leading to the outer hall, the thin top clutched in her hands. Hesitating, she finally reached out with a trembling hand and opened the door a crack, sufficient to let the voices filter through.

"I hope you know what you're doing." At the sound of Pete's voice, Gina's stomach did a sickening somersault.

"I know exactly what I'm doing," Rhyder assured him. There was a faint arrogance in his tone at being questioned. "You just stick to the legal end of this."

"From what you've told me about Justin and what I've seen for myself, I know he isn't going to like it," Pete replied, still unconvinced.

"He doesn't have to like it. He simply has to accept it, and he will," Rhyder said complacently.

"Aren't you being a little premature?" Pete's

skepticism hadn't receded. "You haven't even talked to Gina yet, or so you said."

"After last night, I think I can guarantee that her cooperation is assured." There was a smile in Rhyder's voice, but the sound of it didn't gladden Gina's heart. A tremor of agonizing pain quaked through her. "I've put a call through to my father to tell him the news."

"My God, it isn't even final yet!" came the protest.

"It's only a matter of time and a few signatures on a piece of paper," said Rhyder, dismissing his friend's apprehensive words of caution.

"Yeah, right," Pete agreed in a disgruntled tone, adding a sighing, "I'll talk to you later."

A door closed and Gina guessed that Pete had left the apartment. Quickly she shut the bedroom door, slowly releasing the doorknob so there would be no telltale click of the latch to betray that she had been listening. She walked hurriedly to the center of the room, her heart splintering at the knowledge that Rhyder was using her again.

This time it had been for a twofold purpose—to satisfy the lust she still aroused, and to entrap her with the love he must know she possessed for him and persuade her to convince Justin to agree to Rhyder's terms in the real estate transaction.

Footsteps approached the bedroom. Her back was to it and she quickly pulled the scarlet tunic over her head as it opened. Gina felt his gaze rest on her. For a split second she couldn't move, the sensation was so caressing. She recovered and twisted her hands behind her back to close the zipper.

His long strides eliminated the distance with casual ease. Her hands were pushed out of the way as his fingers took over the task. When it was done, his hands settled firmly on her shoulders.

Then Rhyder bent his dark head to nuzzle the curve of her neck. Gina breathed in deeply, closing her eyes as she tried to brace herself against the evocative caress.

"I was hoping you'd still be in bed," Rhyder murmured against the pulsing vein in her neck.

"I'm glad I'm not," her voice trembled as he found a sensitive point. "I've overslept as it is."

"It's barely nine o'clock." He turned her into his arms. Gina's mind wanted to resist, but her body eagerly allowed him. The brilliant blue light in his eyes weakened her knees. "It isn't an indecent hour to still be in bed."

"You're up," she pointed out, lowering her gaze to the collar of his shirt, starkly white against his mahogany tan. "And dressed."

"Not willingly." His arms slid around her to draw her close. "Pete stopped over early on some business," he explained, and added, "if I'd thought, I would have hung a Do Not Disturb sign on the apartment door and we wouldn't be having this discussion."

"I'm glad you didn't hang out that sign." Her hands were resting on the muscled wall of his chest, wedging a small breathing space for her senses.

Gina was achingly aware that if it hadn't been

for Pete, she wouldn't have known about the way Rhyder intended to abuse her love for him. For the second time in her life, she had been about to make an utter fool of herself over him.

"Why?" He tipped his head back to have a better view of her face.

"Because I'm due in the office. I'm a working girl, remember?" Gina forced the brightness in her answer.

"To hell with the office!" Rhyder slid a hand up to cup her chin, lifting her gaze from its hypnotic study of his shirt front.

His mouth closed over hers with a practiced ease, moistly persuasive as it probed the sweetness of her lips. The icy fear running through her veins had not completely encrusted her heart, and she found herself responding to the flawless technique of his kiss. His arms circled to crush her in an iron band.

He was a master in the art of seduction, and Gina's love made her even more vulnerable to his skill. She fought through the waves of rapture breaking over her senses and surfaced from his kiss, breathing raggedly as she managed to put a few precious inches of sanity between them.

"I have to go to the office," she insisted, staring at his shirt pocket, aware of the uneven rise and fall of his chest.

One arm still half circled her waist while his other hand rested on her rib cage, tantalizingly near the swell of her breast. His head was bent toward hers, his warm breath stirring the raven hair near her temples.

"Call them and tell them you'll be late," Rhyder instructed in a voice husky with desire.

Gina trembled at its message. "I can't do that." She lowered her lashes to hide the contradictory answer in her heart.

Sensing that her resolve was wavering, he lowered his head farther, lightly breathing into her ear and making her flesh tingle as he spoke. "Why not?"

His hand slid to cup the underside of her breast while his thumb began repeating a slow circle over the material covering her nipple until a hard button was formed.

The smooth cheek against her face carried the musky fragrance of after-shave lotion. The heady scent combined with the other erotic stimulants to nearly undermine Gina's will. The searing temptation was there to seek the hardness of his mouth.

With her last ounce of will, she dragged herself away from Rhyder, not stopping until she was several feet away. Sheer luck had directed her to the chair where the matching overblouse was lying.

"I doubt that my clients would understand the reason for my coming in late," she answered his question at last.

"Why tell them?" His low voice was caressing, reaching across the distance to continue his persuasion.

But Gina was far enough away to resist it, although she doubted she would have the determination to resist Rhyder if he followed his words up with more deeds.

"It isn't a question of telling them."

She picked up the blouse and draped it over her arm. She walked toward the door, unable to glance at the tousled covers on the bed or Rhyder. She was already too aware of the sensual undercurrents in the room.

"They consider their appointments with me to be vitally important." He didn't make any attempt to stop her when she walked through the door, only turned to follow. "I can't cancel them simply because...." Gina stumbled over the words that would spell out the reason in stark black and white.

"—because I want to make love to you," Rhyder finished for her.

The self-conscious glance she tossed him over her shoulder quickly ricocheted elsewhere at the knowing glint in his eyes. A faint pink rouged her cheeks at his easy boldness. He was confident of his power over her, and she had given him that power by letting him see the depth of her love last night.

No wonder he had been so certain when he had talked to Pete that he could get her to do whatever he wanted. And he might have if she hadn't overheard the conversation.

"Yes, that's it," she admitted, her footsteps unerringly carrying her into the living room. She spied her briefcase almost instantly. "The reason is a bit selfish."

"Selfish," repeated Rhyder. His gaze never

left her for an instant as she retrieved her brief-case. Now he was between her and the apart-ment door. "After nine years, I don't think it could be described as selfish."

"Perhaps not," she conceded, although she knew his motives were purely selfish.

As she started to walk past him, he caught at her free hand just above the wrist. She stopped, not because of any restraining pressure in his grip but because his touch had the power to steal the strength from her limbs. Her heart rocketed un-der the glittering blue of his gaze.

"There are a lot of other attorneys in the firm you work for, Gina. Let one of them handle the appointment that can't be cancelled," he sug-gested.

His gaze never left her green eyes as he lifted her left hand and turned its palm upward to feel the sensuous caress of his male lips in it center. If it had been love instead of lust that prompted the compelling fire in his gaze, Gina would have agreed without an instant's hesitation.

But it wasn't. "I can't do that." She shook her head, fighting the sensations the hard tip of his tongue was arousing.

"If you were ill, someone would have to take over your clients. Or if there was a family emer-gency. And I'm your husband, Gina, in desper-ate need of you." Rhyder said it lightly but with no less meaning as he turned her hand over and kissed the gold band on her third finger, the ring he had placed there.

"No!" But the gesture nearly made her forget why she was refusing him.

Roughly he pulled her to his side as if he had lost patience with the gentle tactics that had failed to gain him his objective. Bending her left arm behind her back, he arched her against his hip, the hard muscles of his leg sliding between hers.

His mouth closed over hers, parting her lips in hungry demand. Gina was lost to the exploding force of his passion. At her surrender, he released her arm and let his caressing hands melt her flesh as easily as a flame melts wax.

Although her submission was virtually complete, Gina didn't let go of her briefcase, clinging to it tenaciously as if it were her self-respect.

"Gina, call your office and tell them you won't be in—all day," Rhyder ordered against her throat.

Her head was tilted back and to the side, allowing him freer access to the pleasure points along her neck. She glimpsed the gold wedding band on her finger.

Ignoring his command, she asked, "Did you ever tell your parents about me?"

The unexpected question lifted his dark head. A curious frown creased his tanned forehead while an alertness entered his eyes.

"Of course I did," he answered, his mouth twisting into a crooked smile. "That's a strange question. What made you ask?"

"I don't know," Gina breathed. "I guess I was

wondering if I was a skeleton in your family closet."

His head dipped toward her parted lips. "No skeleton in our closet ever had such beautiful bones."

His mouth had barely touched hers when the telephone rang. Rhyder cursed beneath his breath at the interruption. Although partially releasing her, he retained a hold around her waist, drawing her to the telephone with him. He kept her firmly beside him as he picked up the receiver.

Gina was close enough to hear the operator's voice. "We have your party on the line now."

It was his father. She knew instantly, remembering his comment to Pete that he had put a call through to his father. And she knew she didn't have the composure to listen to Rhyder relating the news that he was about to close the deal on the real estate Justin was selling.

Not when he would have to veil the words in sentences where she wasn't supposed to guess the part he was intending her to play in it. Firmly she began to slip from his hold.

"Hello, dad," Rhyder said. "Hold the line a minute." He slid his hand down to cover the mouthpiece as he turned to Gina. "What are you doing?"

"I'm going to the office," she stated.

"I'd forgotten what a stubborn little witch you are," he smiled grimly, but his glance slipped to the telephone receiver in his hand.

"I have work to do." Gina insisted taking

advantage of the fact that he was torn between the desire to speak to his father alone and to have her stay. She glanced at the telephone in his hand. "So do you."

He gave her a long, hard look, then nodded. "All right, I'll see you tonight. I'll pick you up at your office."

"There's no need. I have my own car," she answered, only implying that she was agreeing to see him that night. In truth, she had no intention of it. She couldn't risk it.

As she started to turn away to make good her escape, he caught at her hand, saying, "If you're going to make me work all day at business, the least you can do is kiss me goodbye."

Hesitating, Gina pivoted back, pressing her lips to his for a warm but brief moment. It was more of a goodbye than he knew, and it tore at her heart. She moved quickly out of reach.

Rhyder chuckled softly. "You'll pay for that tonight," he said in warning at the briefness of her kiss. Then the smile faded from his eyes. "Seriously, Gina, we have a lot to talk about tonight as well as a lot of time to make up for."

Not the least among the items to be discussed would be Justin and the terms of the sale, Gina guessed bitterly. She simply smiled wanly in response to his statement and moved hurriedly toward the door. Before she reached it, she heard Rhyder speaking into the telephone.

"Sorry to keep you waiting, dad, but Gina was here. . . . Yes, she's just leaving."

The rest of the conversation was lost to Gina as

she stepped into the hallway and closed the door. It wasn't until she was outside that she realized she had no means of transportation. Her car was still parked in the lot near her office.

She paused beside an outdoor telephone booth, debating whether or not to call a taxi, before deciding that a brisk walk in the sharp September air was just what she needed to blow away the cobwebs spun by her emotions.

It was rather startling to hear the birds singing. She felt so dead inside. A scattering of leaves on the maple trees was tinged with crimson. To most, it would have been an indication of the autumn spectacle that approached the Maine flora. But the blood red shade only reminded Gina of the deep wound in her heart.

When she arrived at the office, she felt somewhat better from the long walk. Her heartache hadn't been resolved, but her determination not to let Rhyder use her had been strengthened. During the day Justin telephoned her twice, each time insisting it was urgent, but Gina didn't accept the calls.

She dismissed the urgency of his calls with the reasoning that Rhyder wouldn't approach him until he had his discussion with her. And he still didn't know the discussion would never take place.

A few minutes before five o'clock, Gina hurried from the office building. Despite her assurances to Rhyder that he needn't pick her up, she was half afraid he would be waiting for her. She made it to her car without anyone trying to stop her.

But she knew it wasn't over. There was still tonight. When she didn't arrive at his apartment, she knew Rhyder would telephone. And when she didn't answer the phone, which she wouldn't, he would come over.

Even if she did answer the telephone, Gina knew he would never accept her refusal to see him and would come to her apartment anyway. When he did come, she would call the police. She would have no other choice. She didn't dare listen to him; she was too susceptible to his brand of persuasion.

Her plans were well thought out and certain to succeed in keeping her from any direct contact with Rhyder, but Gina didn't feel any sense of triumph when she arrived at her apartment building. She loved him and wanted only his love in return, but to be used was more than her stiff-necked Yankee pride —a trait she had inherited from her grandfather—could bear.

Melancholy deadened her footsteps as she approached the door to her apartment and rummaged through her handbag for the key. She inserted it in the lock, turned it and pushed, but the door didn't budge. She tried it again with no success, then self-consciously double-checked to be certain she hadn't accidentally stopped at the wrong door.

It was her apartment, but the key wouldn't work in the lock. She doubled-checked to be sure she had the right key. She did.

Puzzled, she retraced her steps to the front part of the building where the resident manager lived. She knocked at the door. It opened a crack, a safety chain keeping it from opening all the way. Gina smiled politely at the housecoated woman peering at her.

"I'm sorry to disturb you, Mrs. Powell, but I can't seem to get my key to work. Could you use your passkey to let me into my apartment?" she requested.

The chain remained in place while the woman tipped back her head to peer at Gina through the half-moon lenses of her glasses, as if trying to place her. The pinched lines around her mouth softened slightly in recognition.

"Of course your key won't work," the elderly woman declared. "The man's already come to change the lock."

A winged brow arched briefly in surprise. Then Gina sighed. She supposed the notice had been slipped in her mailbox, but she hadn't checked it in several days. The only time she ever received mail of any importance was the first of the month when the bills arrived.

She had had no close family since her grandfather died, and correspondence with her school friends had long since ended. The locks had probably been as a precaution of some sort.

"Could I have the new set of keys?" she asked patiently.

"Why?" the woman wanted to know, straightening her hunched shoulders slightly.

"To get into my apartment, of course," Gina

replied, exhaling a disbelieving laugh at the question.

"T'wouldn't be any reason to give 'em to you. There's nothin' in it that belongs to you," Mrs. Powell declared.

"What?" An open frown of bewilderment covered Gina's face as she tried to fathom this mysterious conversation.

"Everything's packed and gone. There's nothin' left there that's yours," the woman repeated in a louder tone, as if Gina were deaf.

"Gone where?" Gina demanded.

"Well, dearie, you're the one who should know where. It's not my business," the woman nodded.

"Well, I don't know where," Gina answered, her patience receding. "If somebody has taken my things, then it was without my permission. Would you mind letting me come in, Mrs. Powell, so I can phone the police?"

"The police? Why should you want to call them?" The woman frowned. "There was nothin' stolen. Your husband supervised the packin' of nearly everything himself."

"My husband?" Gina breathed in sharply. It all became suddenly very clear.

"Yes, your husband. You don't think I'd just let anybody into your apartment and take your things?" Mrs. Powell sniffed indignantly.

"Of course not," Gina acknowledged grudgingly, her lips compressed in anger.

All her well-laid plans were nothing. Rhyder

had been so confident that he had moved her out lock, stock, and barrel. A slow anger set in.

"I explained to your husband that you still had four months left on your lease and a month's notice was required before vacating," the woman continued. "He paid for the rest of the lease and added another month's rent in lieu of notice. He took care of everything for you."

"Yes, I can see that," Gina nodded grimly.

"If there's nothing else ...." There was a pregnant pause as the woman silently indicated that Gina was taking up her time needlessly.

"No. No, nothing else," Gina agreed after a second's hesitation. "I'm sorry to have troubled you, Mrs. Powell."

"That's quite all right." The door started to close, the chain slackening. It straightened again as the manageress added as an afterthought, "And congratulations, too. You have a fine man there."

Gina didn't respond to that as she turned on her heel, her temper simmering. She was saving the scalding fury of her anger for Rhyder. Its impetus carried her swiftly to her car.

CHAPTER NINE

COLD RAGE FILLED HER as Gina paused in front of Rhyder's apartment door. Her sharp, impatient knock echoed the pounding of her heart against her ribs. Within seconds the door swung open and Rhyder was facing her. A smile of lazy beguilement spread across the rugged planes of his tanned features.

"It's about time you got here," he declared warmly, reaching out to grasp the rigid mucles of her arms and draw her inside. "I was about to send out a search party for you."

Closing the door, he started to pull her the rest of the way into his embrace. Stiffly Gina resisted, her seething temper keeping her immune to his possessive touch.

"Just where did you think I might go?" The question came out in a low rush of harsh accusation that slowly straightened the curve of his mouth. "You made certain I had nowhere else!"

A smiling gleam remained in the brilliant blue of his eyes, crinkling at the corners as he gazed deeply into her green ones. The hands gripping her shoulders didn't force her nearer, nor did they let her go.

"The last time I saw the ocean look that way, it

was building to a storm," Rhyder commented, referring to the turbulent shade of green in her eyes. "Did you have a rough day?"

Gina breathed in sharply, enraged that he could pretend to be so dense that he didn't know. He wasn't fooling her for a second. He knew very well why she was angry.

"I want to know where the things are from my apartment," she demanded.

"Your clothes are in the bedroom. There are some boxes of things in the spare room that I wasn't sure what you wanted to do with, and the odds and ends of furniture I had stored for the time being," Rhyder answered with leisurely ease.

"Who gave you the right to do anything with my things?" Gina challenged, incensed that he could so calmly admit to what he had done.

"So that's what you're so upset about." He smiled softly as he understood the cause of her anger. His hands began slowly massaging her shoulders and arms with a caressively stroking motion while his gaze ran possessively over her face, a smoldering light of banked desire in the look. "I probably should have let you know," he conceded, "but I wanted to surprise you."

"Surprise me!" Gina choked on the audacity of the bland claim.

"It's been my experience that women take an eternity of time sorting and packing to move and repeat practically the whole process when it's time to unpack. Experience gained from observing my mother and sister," he added, as if to assure her he had helped no other woman to move. "I decided that if I told you I was having a moving company come, you'd be there fussing around and it would take twice as long. Now it's all done and you don't have to be concerned about it."

"Well, you can just call up your precious moving company and have everything moved back!" she stormed.

His gaze narrowed, a quietness stealing over him "Were you planning to maintain a separate residence?"

"A residence permanently separated from you!" Gina declared, and pulled away from his touch to further enforce her determination to have no part of him or his life.

Rhyder didn't try to reestablish physical contact with her, yet there remained a coiled watchfulness about him, indicating that any moment he could change his mind and strike. The air was charged between them, lightning tongues of tension licking her spine.

"I think you'd better explain that remark," he said in that dangerously quiet voice.

"I don't see what there is to explain," she retorted defiantly. "I thought it was perfectly clear. I am going to live in my apartment and you are going to live wherever else you choose. Your high-handed tactics of canceling my lease and moving my things out simply aren't going to work."

"I told you—" a muscle was flexing in his neck "—I was trying to be considerate. I wanted us to have time together instead of spending half of it moving you here."

Gina tossed her head in arrogant challenge. "When did I ever say that I wanted to live with you?"

His expression hardened. "You didn't in so many words," he admitted, "but last night your actions spoke for themselves."

"You assumed wrong!" she flashed.

"Are you going to try to convince me now that you didn't want to stay with me last night? That I forced you to?" His lips curled in a cynical jeer.

Her cheeks reddened as she replied angrily, "No, I'm not! But I never indicated that I wanted it to be a permanent arrangement!"

"You are my wife!" Rhyder snapped. "You belong to me!"

"I am Gina Gaynes and I belong to no one but myself!" His arrogant claim of possession incited her to deny that any part of her belonged to him, even though she knew she had given him her heart.

"Damn it," he muttered beneath his breath, "I knew I should never have let you leave this morning."

The words were barely out before his hand snaked forward to grip her wrist with the striking swiftness of a cobra. Her reaction was too slow to elude him. Violently Rhyder yanked her toward him. In defense, Gina's arm swung, the flat of her hand connecting with his cheek. The hard contact sent shock waves of pain rolling through her arm.

Instantly the striking hand was seized and twisted with the other behind her back to crush her against the granite wall of his chest. His expression was dark with anger as he glared at her whitened face.

"How many times do you think you can slap my face without receiving retribution?" he snarled.

Gina strained and twisted to break free, fearing his manner of punishment. He shifted his grip, a single iron band pinning her to him while his fingers twisted into her raven hair, pulling at the tender roots until the pain forced Gina to be still. The pain had barely eased in her scalp when her lips were ground against her teeth by his vengeful mouth.

Reeling under his punitive assault, Gina tried to struggle, but it only served to feed his wrath. The air was soon crushed from her lungs by the constricting band of his arm. His smothering kiss refused to let her draw new breath. Blackness swirled behind her tightly closed eyes. The rigidity of her body, which was her only remaining gesture of resistance, wilted with her ebbing strength.

With the last bastion of her resistance conquered, Rhyder set out to taste the spoils of his victory, searching relentlessly for the sweetness of her lips, plundering their softness. The ravaging fire of his kiss sparked the quivering beginnings of a response.

The fingers curling through her hair were no longer inflicting pain. Before Gina found herself surrending to his hungry demand for passion, she valiantly twisted away from the hard male lips.

"Let me go!" Gulping in air, her voice was breathy and low. "Or do you intend to exercise your husbandly rights by raping me?" Her face was turned far to the side away from him.

"Damn you, Gina." The savage groan was breathed against the arching curve of her neck. "You always seem to manage to make me despise myself for the way I feel, and half the time I'm only responding to your invitations."

"Let me go," she repeated, aware that he spoke the truth.

Her senses were clamoring from the musky male scent enveloping her and the hard feel of his body pressed against hers. Rhyder lifted his head slightly to study her averted profile, the moist warmth of his breath caressing her cheek and the sensitive skin along her neck.

"How, Gina?" he demanded in a husky pitch. "How do I let you go? I can't. Not yet."

No, her heart cried in pain, he couldn't let her go until he had accomplished his objective of buying the property on his terms, not Justin's. For that, he needed her. In the meantime he would use her to satisfy the lust she aroused in him. And that wasn't enough. To settle for that would literally break her.

Extreme tiredness washed through her. Gina fought it as she fought the emotional upsurge of her love for Rhyder. Both could too easily be turned into weapons against her. She strained against his arms.

"You can't hold me prisoner," she declared in a low voice to hide her weariness.

"Why not?" he mocked with a sardonic inflection. "For nine years, your memory kept me its prisoner. Now I'm holding the real thing. I can feel the beat of your heart, the heat of your body, the softness of your flesh against mine. Why should I only remember when I can hold what's mine?"

"I am not yours and I never will be," Gina continued to protest, deafening her ears to his seductive words. "So let me go!"

Rhyder allowed her to move a foot away, retaining a firm hold on her arms to prevent her from escaping altogether. The metallic hardness of his gaze was like a steel bit boring into her.

"I'm not letting you. Not until we've talked this out." The qualification was the first sign that her adamancy was gaining her ground.

"There's nothing to talk out," she stated. "The only thing I want from you is to have my belongings returned to my apartment and to be left alone, so there's nothing to discuss."

"Yes, there is," returned Rhyder in a voice that was positive and unrelenting in its purpose. "We're going to talk about the way you've changed from what you were this morning and last night to the way you are now."

"It would be pointless." Exhaustion was setting in again. She was tired of constantly having to struggle to protect herself, mentally as well as physically.

"I disagree," he denied flatly, indicating that

he would accept no other conditions for her release.

Her wan complexion came from her inner weariness of fighting. Her eyes, a faintly haunted green, beseeched him silently not to put her through this, although her pride would not let her verbalize her plea.

The male line of his lips tightened. The creases on either side of his mouth were carved deeper as his searching gaze narrowed on her face and its brief expression of vulnerability and hurt. A slight frown creased his forehead.

"Gina . . . " Rhyder began, vaguely questioning, his hands tightening on her as if to draw her to him and show her the comfort of his strong arms.

A knock at the apartment door checked his movement. His frown changed to one of irritation at the interruption. The second knock drew his impatient glance, and Gina was released from his compelling gaze, gaining the respite she needed to reestablish the firmness of her stand. Rhyder sensed the change immediately, the line of his jaw hardening.

He let his hands drop to his sides. "We aren't finished," he stated sharply. It was more of a threat than a warning as he left Gina to walk to the door.

A silent sigh of apprehension quivered through her. Her skin felt chilled where his hands had held her. She wondered how much more she could endure without breaking up.

While her mind was wondering about that, her

senses were following Rhyder, listening to his footsteps and the opening of the door. The blood froze in her veins when she heard him greet the caller.

"Hello, Justin. What is it you want?" The clipped demand by Rhyder made it plain that Justin wasn't welcome.

Gina pivoted slowly toward the door. Her harrowed eyes met the harshly accusing look Justin gave her over Rhyder's shoulder. He exhibited not the slightest surprise at seeing her there. The remaining color drained from her cheeks.

"I was told," Justin stated coldly, his gaze slicing to Rhyder, "that I could find Gina here."

Seconds ticked by in silence, the tension heightening to a charged level as Rhyder stood in the doorway, blocking Justin's entrance. Slowly, like an uncoiling spring, Rhyder appeared to relax as he stepped to the side.

"Yes, she's here," he agreed, stating the obvious since he knew Justin could see Gina standing in the foyer of the living room. "Would you like to speak to her?"

"Please," Justin answered stiffly, and walked into the apartment.

As Rhyder closed the door behind him, his gaze slid to Gina's white face, then returned to Justin, whose attention was darting between the two. Rhyder's mouth curved into an aloofly courteous smile.

"I was about to fix Gina a drink. Would you like one, Justin?" he inquired.

Justin was on the point of refusing when he glanced at Gina and changed his mind. "Scotch and water," he said, accepting the offer.

Gina stared numbly at Rhyder, surprised that he had invited Justin in and offered him a drink. An inner sense told her that initially Rhyder had wanted to get rid of Justin as soon as he could, not welcoming the interruption from a man he possibly regarded as a rival.

Her gaze searched his impassive expression for a reason, but Rhyder barely glanced at her as he walked by her into the living room and to the small bar located at the far end.

Her attention was forced to refocus on Justin. With her nerves stretched thin, Gina made a futile attempt to smile, seeking to pretend the situation was natural.

"I've been trying to reach you all day." The low volume of Justin's voice didn't lessen the accusation in the statement.

"Yes, I know," Gina admitted, adding in false apology, "I'm sorry I wasn't able to return your calls, but I was tied up most of the day."

His brown eyes glowered their disbelief. "I see," Justin said grimly. "You were so busy you couldn't even spare five minutes to return my calls, is that what you're saying?"

"Yes." Rigidly clinging to her lie, Gina turned to enter the beige living room.

Her step faltered at Justin's angrily low and demanding, "Aren't you going to ask how I found out you were here?"

Perhaps it was his unjustified anger or his

willingness to believe that things were as they seemed that turned Gina against him. Any thought of looking on him as an ally to stand beside her against Rhyder vanished at his silent condemnation.

"How did you find out, Justin?" Gina asked the question he had prompted with icy calm.

"I went to your apartment to find you and the woman that manages the building told me you'd moved out. Your husband—" he underlined the word "—had moved your things."

"I thought that was how you learned I was here," she responded evenly.

"I couldn't believe it was true," Justin muttered in a bitter breath. "I kept telling myself that the stupid old woman had got it wrong. I had to come to see for myself if you'd gone back to him."

"And now you're here." Gina lifted her chin, pale and proud, as she prompted him to say what was in his expression.

"And I see." His mouth tightened.

Gina knew that she had deliberately let him believe she had gone back to Rhyder, both by her words and her actions. But she couldn't let him go on thinking that way.

"Appearances are deceptive." She began her explanation stiffly. "I know how it seems to you, Justin, but it isn't true."

His head was drawn back to study her. "Are you saying that you haven't gone back to Rhyder?" he asked warily.

As her lips parted to state unequivocally that

she hadn't, Rhyder's tall shape entered her side vision and he was answering the question before she had the chance.

"That was under discussion when you arrived, Justin. Scotch and water." He offered a squat glass to Justin, cubes of ice glistening in the pale gold liquid. The glass in his other hand he extended to Gina, the glittering light in his eyes holding her gaze. "My wife's moods are as changeable as the ocean. Our reconciliation is barely twenty-four hours old and already it's in jeopardy."

His words hung suspended in the air, carrying the charged undercurrents of a high-voltage wire. Automatically Justin had accepted the drink offered him, but his limbs were frozen by Rhyder's deliberate intimation that they had shared at least one night's worth of reconciliation.

A red flush of shame and anger rose in Gina's cheeks. She couldn't deny the truth and Ryder knew it. Again she was subjected to the harsh sweep of condemnation in Justin's gaze, while Rhyder's expression remained aloof yet mockingly complacent. Her failure to deny Rhyder's implication spoke as loudly as if she had confirmed it.

The urge rose to slap the proffered drink from Rhyder's hand. The blaze of temper must have flashed in her eyes, because Rhyder's gaze narrowed faintly in warning. He grasped her hand and curled her resisting fingers around the cold glass.

"I don't want it," she refused.

"Drink it," Rhyder ordered. "It will help settle your nerves." He released the hand he had forced to hold the glass and slipped a proprietorial arm around her waist to turn her to the center of the living room. He seemed unconcerned that Gina might fling the contents of the glass in his face. Strangely, she found she couldn't do it, although she wanted to. "Have a seat, Justin," Rhyder invited as he led Gina to the sofa and forced her to sit beside him.

Hesitating, Justin lifted his glass, downing a large swallow of his drink as if his system needed the reviving jolt of liquor. Then he walked to an armchair near the sofa and sat down, his sullen gaze sweeping over both of them.

"Gina's things are here," Justin said in a tone that requested clarification of the statement.

"Only temporarily," Gina answered.

"Yes, they are here," Rhyder asserted, making it sound as if they would never leave, and Gina flashed him an angry look of denial.

Justin stared at the cubes floating in his glass. "You should have told me, Gina," he said grimly, "instead of letting me believe that you despised him."

"Ours has always been a stormy relationship," Rhyder responded to the comment when Gina failed to find her voice, "with equal portions of anger and passion in between the dormant periods. You've happened to see us together in our more angered moments, such as now."

"Gina had said you weren't married, that the

two of you were divorced." Justin seemed prepared for Rhyder's answer.

"A slight exaggeration," he shrugged. "We'd been separated for several years, so it was only natural that she should think along those lines."

"And I still do!" Gina snapped, irritated by the way they were conversing as if she weren't around and neither of them had any particular interest in the subject.

Rhyder glanced down, his features set in uncompromising lines as he studied the mutinous glint in her eyes. "That's something we will discuss in private."

Words trembled on her lips to deny that being alone with him would make any difference to her decision, but she was afraid it would. She had to look away from the masculine features, so hard and angular, that she had come to love more deeply than the sixteen-year-old girl had ever loved. Tears burned the back of her eyes.

Rhyder's fingers closed around the hand holding her drink and lifted it to carry the glass to her lips. "Drink it," he ordered quietly, sensing how near her nerves were to total collapse.

For an instant Gina resisted the command, but the silent presence of his strength finally had her obey. The drink burned her throat, made her choke in its fire, but it allowed the true cause of her glistening tears to be disguised in the reaction. She could only hope that Rhyder hadn't guessed the reason behind her initial weakness and trembling.

"What about my property, Rhyder?" Justin

broke the silence that had accompanied Gina's recovery. "Are you still interested in it?"

Gina could almost see Rhyder withdraw behind an emotionless mask that revealed nothing. She waited, feeling the tension build inside of her.

"That depends," he answered noncommittally.

"On what?" Justin persisted.

"On some other related matters." Rhyder explained nothing, but Gina knew exactly what he had left unsaid.

An encompassing hurt scraped over her nerve ends, leaving them raw and frayed. In her pain she decided to let Rhyder know she was aware of his plans to make use of her in his dealings with Justin.

"What he means, Justin—" the tenor of her voice was rigidly controlled "—is that it depends on me and what I decide. Isn't that correct, Rhyder?" She challenged him to deny it.

He studied her for a silent second in aloof contemplation, a dark eyebrow twisting slightly, but it was to Justin that he directed his words.

"Yes, Gina is right. My answer will depend on her decision," Rhyder agreed calmly.

She hadn't expected him to admit it. He had so carefully avoided giving any indication that he wanted more from Gina than to have her live with him as his wife. Perhaps Rhyder had finally realized that she wasn't so easily fooled.

Justin exhaled a heavy breath and drained the liquid in his glass, setting it on the table with an air of finality. He rose to his feet, his measured brown gaze seeking Rhyder.

"How long am I to wait for your answer?" he asked.

"Gina will give me her final answer tonight, one way or the other." Rhyder straightened, his gaze flicking briefly to Gina. "You will have mine in the morning."

Justin nodded his understanding and acceptance. "Since I have a personal as well as a business stake in the outcome, I'd better leave now. My staying here is only delaying the process," he concluded.

As he turned to leave, Gina realized that she was about to let her chance escape for a safe escort from Rhyder's apartment. She had made her decision. Rhyder knew what it was, but he hoped to change it. And Gina wasn't sure she could insulate her heart against his persuasions.

Hurriedly she rose from the sofa, setting her glass on a table, and took a step after Justin. His name became lodged in her throat as Rhyder's hands gripped the soft flesh of her arms and drew her shoulders back to his chest.

"Stay." The one word was quietly spoken near her ear, his warm breath gently stirring her hair.

Gina's resolve weakened in compliance with his command. She let Rhyder hold her there as Justin paused by the door to glance back. The dull look in his brown eyes seemed to concede the victory to Rhyder. Momentarily caught in the spell of his touch, Gina couldn't deny it.

When the door closed, his hands slid down to

her forearms, curling them across the front of her waist as he curved her more fully against him. His mouth sought the sensitive nape of her neck, sending quivers of desire over her skin. His caress had the power to seduce her will, and she strained her neck away, pushing herself free.

"Why did you do it?" she demanded breathlessly, her hands pressed against her rapidly fluttering stomach.

"Do what?" Rhyder asked her, seeking to draw her into his embrace again.

But Gina pivoted away, maintaining a breathing distance as she faced him. Her green eyes were rounded and warily bright through the sweeping curl of her lashes.

"Why did you invite Justin in? Why did you have to involve him directly in this?" She bombarded him with questions to keep him at a distance, the protective words rushing from her lips. "And why the pose of civility, pretending a courtesy you know you didn't feel?"

"What would you have preferred?" he asked curtly. "Should we have brawled? Is that what you wanted? Did you want to see us fight over you?"

"No, of course not!" Gina retorted, knowing he had deliberately twisted her questions.

"Good!" Rhyder snapped. "Because it would have been an exercise in futility. The woman always ends up choosing who she wants regardless of who wins or loses. To fight over you would have been pointless, because it wouldn't have influenced your choice."

"You are right," Gina conceded tightly. "And you know my decision. You aren't going to change my mind. You're wasting your time trying-ing."

"Why, Gina?" It was Rhyder who demanded answers, towering before her, intimidating her with the force of his personality. "Why are you telling me no after coming to me so willingly last night?"

She searched wildly for an answer. "Did it ever occur to you that I might be exorcising a ghost of nine years? Ridding myself of the memory of a sixteen-year-old's infatuation?"

"It wasn't a memory I held in my arms." Rhyder dismissed the suggestion swiftly.

"Maybe after sleeping with you, I discovered I preferred Justin," Gina challenged desperately.

Although Rhyder didn't move, he seemed to loom nearer, his fury rising over her like a tidal wave. Gina felt the drowning force of its undertow. A muscle leaped uncontrollably in his jaw. The atmosphere was electrified as Rhyder controlled his anger with an effort.

"If I believed you meant that—" his voice vibrated deep in his throat, harsh and raw "—I think I'd . . . ."

He didn't finish the rest. He didn't need to. Gina could almost feel his strangling fingers around her neck. Shivering, she knew she had provoked him without thought of the consequences.

"Does it matter whether something happened last night or nine years ago?" she asked quietly.

"It still doesn't change the fact that I want to be free of you."

"Why?" Rhyder demanded again.

"Because—" her dark head moved despairingly to the side "—I just don't want to spend the rest of my life with you." The heartbreak would be unendurable, with the knowledge that he didn't love her and was only using her. "So please, just let me go,"

An angered frustration swept across Rhyder's features as he tried to find a fallacy in her words and failed. He breathed in deeply, his unwillingness to accept her statement as obvious as his inability to argue against it.

"Is that your final word?" he questioned at last, low and impatient.

"Yes." Gina held her breath. Praying that her torment might be at an end.

Raking fingers through the ebony thickness of his hair, Rhyder pivoted away. "Why? Why? Why?" Drawn through clenched teeth, the words weren't directed at Gina. They were an angered demand to the fates.

There was a knock at the door and Gina jumped convulsively at the sound. Her gaze flew to Rhyder, who had reacted with the same degree of surprise. She didn't want another interruption. He was about to let her go. She sensed that, and didn't want the moment prolonged. Time was working against her. Rhyder's gaze sliced to her with the fine edge of cutting steel.

Another knock, more impatient than the first, ripped his pinning gaze from her. Swearing beneath his breath, Rhyder's long strides carried him toward the door. Gina's hands were twisted so tightly together there was hardly any circulation flowing through her fingers.

He swung the door open, controlled violence in his movement. His arm was braced against the door frame to block the entrance. Gina knew that if it was Justin who had returned, he would not gain admittance this time.

CHAPTER TEN

WITH ONE GLANCE at the person in the hall,
Rhyder flung the door open and walked away.
His action stunned Gina until she saw an equally
surprised Pete following in his wake.

"If you can't give me a 'hello,' how about
offering me a drink?" Pete said with a short,
bewildered laugh. Then he noticed Gina and
smiled. "I didn't think you'd be here—which just
shows that a celebration is definitely in order."

"Save it, Pete," Rhyder snapped as he walked
to the bar.

"W-what?" Pete cocked his sandy head, only
that instant picking up the electrical tension
crackling around Rhyder.

"There's nothing to celebrate." Rhyder's lips
twisted with bitter cynicism as he added, "Unless you want to toast the fact that you were
right."

"You mean—" Pete's gaze swerved to Gina,
widening as he observed the pinched lines of
strain in her pale face "—that . . . ." He hesitated,
reluctant to say the obvious.

"—Gina has said no," Rhyder finished it, his
voice taut and low.

Already in the living room, Pete virtually

dropped into the armchair recently vacated by Justin. There was no elation at being right as a grimly resigned Pete reached into the inner pocket of his jacket and pulled out a sheaf of papers.

"And I just spent the whole day running all over half the state of Maine for nothing," he sighed, and tossed the papers on the table a few feet in front of the chair.

Rhyder walked from the bar and handed him the drink he had mixed, glancing briefly at the papers. "Then you got it?" he commented.

"Yes," Pete nodded glumly. "All signed, sealed and legal."

Gina's gaze darted from one to the other, faintly puzzled by their exchange. Rhyder flicked a look at her, the raking glance taking in the questing light in her green eyes. He moved to the sofa.

"You might as well sit down, Gina," he said crisply.

Numbly she moved to a twin chair of Pete's. "What are you talking about?"

Pete met her eyes reluctantly. "I had the annulment ruling officially voided. Your marriage to Rhyder legally exists on a technicality. I thought the two of you had patched things up," he explained, implying that he knew about last night.

"You were mistaken." Gina lowered her gaze, feeling the heat warming her cheeks.

"It's a pity." Pete sipped absently at his drink. "Rhyder was so positive."

"I changed my mind," she muttered. "It's my prerogative."

"Do you mind if I ask why?" The lenses of his glasses intensified the gentle light in Pete's eyes when he glanced at her.

Rhyder answered the question with harsh flatness. "Gina can't stand the thought of living with me for the rest of her life."

"That's certainly a valid reason. You wouldn't be my choice, either." Pete tried to make a joke of it, but nobody laughed.

Leaning forward on the sofa cushion, Rhyder leaned his elbows on his knees, his hands clasped loosely in front of him. He stared at them, tiredness etched in the curve of his broad shoulders and the slightly bowed neck.

"What's the next move, Pete?" he asked dispiritedly.

His tone suggested that he didn't really care and the question was asked because the world wouldn't stop to let him off. Gina knew the feeling. She felt it more intensely than Rhyder did because she loved him. He was only reacting to the fact that his plans were beyond salvage.

"Well—" Pete breathed in deeply, held it for a split second as he glanced hesitantly at Gina, and let it out "—I don't suppose you would agree to a few months' trial period to see if the two of you could make the marriage work?"

"No!" Gina rejected the idea almost violently, then added on a more controlled note, "All I want is for Rhyder to let me go and to send my things back to my apartment."

"Your things?" A sandy eyebrow lifted above the frames of Pete's glasses.

"Yes," she nodded. "Rhyder canceled the lease on my apartment today and had everything moved here." But she couldn't summon her former anger at Rhyder's arrogant manipulations.

"Good lord!" Pete breathed, and sat back in his chair staring at Rhyder, amazed at his audacity. "You really did anticipate her decision, didn't you?"

"I thought I had cause," Rhyder muttered, rising impatiently to his feet and rubbing the back of his neck. "I should have guessed that she'd turned into a permissive little witch hopping in and out of—"

"That's not true!" Gina protested angrily. "I've never—"

"Now, now," Pete interrupted, his hands spread to halt her indignant rush. "This situation isn't going to be helped if the two of you start shouting and calling each other names."

Rigidly Rhyder turned his back to her, moving to the far side of the room and the bar. His wounding words still stung, but Gina pressed her lips together.

Glancing from one to the other, Pete smiled briefly in satisfaction. "Good. Now let's start tackling this situation one step at a time. The immediate problem is your apartment, Gina. I'll go over first thing tomorrow morning and get the lease straightened out. As soon as it is, I'll have your belongings moved back. In the meantime, you'll have to get a motel room for the night. Agreed?"

"Yes," she nodded, achingly aware of Rhyder slowly pacing the confines of the living room.

"The next order of business would be the separation papers." Pete took a small notebook and pen from an inside pocket of his jacket. His head was bent as he started to make notes. He flicked a quick, confirming look at Gina over the top frame of his glasses. "I presume you will be the one filing the divorce papers?"

Her heart constricted as she nodded again. "Yes."

"No!" Rhyder barked, stopping near her chair.

"On what grounds?" Pete continued.

"I don't know." Gina shook her head, her pulse racing in the crackling atmosphere as she tried to ignore Rhyder. "Incompatibility, I suppose," she shrugged.

"You are not filing for a divorce," Rhyder stated in a threatening tone.

His nearness seemed to almost crush her. In agitation, Gina rose to her feet. Seated, she had found his height advantage had been too overpowering. Her knees trembled with traitorous weakness as she stood before him, trying to summon a defensive anger.

"Then you file for the divorce!" she retorted. "It doesn't matter to me."

"I'm not giving you a divorce!" he snapped.

Frozen by his declaration, Gina couldn't elude the hands that reached out to grip her shoulders punishingly. His rugged features were carved in unyielding lines, the piercing blue of his gaze impaling her.

"You're not getting rid of me as easily as you did nine years ago." His warning was a promise. "There will be no divorce."

Gina breathed in sharply. "No!" Tears welled in her eyes, shimmering with emerald brilliance.

The sight of them tightened his mouth, snapping something inside of him. She was jerked roughly to his chest, her hands raised instinctively to press against the solid wall in protest even as her flesh melted to the hard feel of his length.

His head bent near her ear, his face partially buried in the soft raven hair. Gina had to close her eyes to the searing longings his touch evoked.

"You're my wife, Gina," Rhyder muttered harshly. "I'm not letting you go."

The torture of loving him and having to deny the love was revealed in her expression. She didn't try to hide it because she knew Rhyder couldn't see it. Pete did. Closing his notebook, he settled back in his chair as Gina found the strength to twist free.

"I'm filing for a divorce, Rhyder." Gina repeated the statement to reassure herself of her intentions. She kept her face averted from Rhyder until she felt a semblance of control return.

"I'll fight it," he stated.

"Let's not be hasty, Rhyder." Pete tipped his head to one side in a considering gesture and felt the thrust of Rhyder's gaze.

"You are my lawyer, Pete," Rhyder said tautly, "and I'm ordering you to contest any action Gina takes in the divorce courts. When I want your advice, I'll ask for it. Don't give me any of it until I do."

"I'm just suggesting that I think we should sit down and discuss this rationally instead of continually getting sidetracked by emotions," Pete replied, letting the outburst slide over him. "I'm sure Gina agrees with me, don't you?"

"Yes," she agreed shakily.

Turning away, Rhyder seemed to grimly dissociate himself from the talk. Hands twisted in her lap, Gina sat on the edge of her chair.

"What were you thinking of in terms of a divorce settlement?" Pete asked.

"I want a divorce, nothing more," Gina insisted huskily.

Rhyder exhaled a short, contemptous breath. "That's a first!"

His stinging words prompted a low retort. "I never wanted any money from you before. You wanted to pay it to clear your conscience and I took it because I thought you owed it to me. We were both mistaken."

"The court will probably award a token settlement to you," Pete commented, and sighed. "It could have all been very simple."

"It won't be," Rhyder snapped. "Whether there's a settlement involved or not, I'm fighting the divorce."

"I was referring to the fact that it would have been simpler if it hadn't been for your reconciliation, however brief it was," Pete explained, quietly studying Rhyder's back. "It would have been a matter of mere paperwork."

But Gina was being ripped by Rhyder's adamant insistence that he would contest any action to dissolve their marriage. "Why are you doing this?" she demanded desperately. "I'm only asking to be free of you, nothing more. Why? Tell me why"

"Yes, Rhyder." Pete unexpectedly endorsed her question. "Gina is being more than cooperative about the divorce. Tell us why you aren't."

"Damn it, Pete! You know the answer to that!" Rhyder pivoted to face his friend, obviously angry that the question had been asked.

Her shoulders drooped slightly as Gina sighed, "So do I."

Pete eyed her curiously. "If you do then why did you ask?"

"Because—" she lifted her chin, but her gaze remained on the whitened knuckles of his twisting hands "—I thought that under the circumstances Rhyder would have given up his plans to use me to get the property."

"What property?" came Rhyder's low demand, ominously soft and swift.

"You know very well what property." She flashed him a look of irritation.

"Would you mind telling me?" Pete glanced from one to the other, settling finally on Gina.

"Justin's property, of course," she answered tightly.

"What?" Rhyder's voice was tautly thin with angry astonishment.

Pete's sandy head was drawn back, the light in his eyes thoughtfully remote as he studied her defiant expression. "What were his plans?"

"I'm sure he discussed it with you," Gina retorted in a caustic tone.

A sound started to come from Rhyder, low and angry, but Pete flicked him a silencing look and and returned the focus of his attention to Gina.

"No, I don't believe he did," he replied calmly. "Would you fill me in?"

"He was hoping to charm me into persuading Justin to sell on his terms." Her lips were compressed tightly for an instant. "Now I suppose he's going to make it a condition before he'll agree to the divorce."

"Of all the—" Rhyder's explosion was halted by Pete's upraised hand.

"Are you sure about this?" Pete studied her intently.

"Yes, I'm sure." Gina wished she wasn't. "He admitted it when Justin was here a half an hour ago."

"That's a lie!" Rhyder denied savagely.

Gina flinched at his angered and false disclaimer and continued. "It's true. You told Justin your decision to buy the property would depend on me," she reminded him coldly. "Besides, I overheard you talking to Pete this morning."

"What has that got to do with it?" Pete asked in surprise.

"Have you forgotten?" she retorted bitterly.

"Rhyder told you he could practically guarantee my cooperation, regardless of whether Justin liked it or not. He even called his father to prematurely give him the news that he was about to get the property on his terms, even though he hadn't talked to me."

"And you thought—" Pete began, a smile widening his mouth.

"Never mind!" Rhyder snapped the interruption. "Give me the land contract proposal Gina drew up."

The smile didn't fade as Pete reached for the briefcase resting against his chair. Opening it, he leafed through the papers and handed a stapled set to Rhyder. Gina watched, waiting for the tanned fingers to tear the papers in two now that Rhyder realized she wouldn't be coerced into agreeing with his scheme.

Her green eyes widened in confusion as she saw him affix his signature to the proposal. Immediately he thrust the papers and pen toward Pete.

"Witness it," he ordered curtly. When it was done he shoved it into Gina's hands. "Here's your precious agreement, accepted, signed and witnessed—on Justin's terms!"

"I—" numbly she lifted her gaze to the thunderous mask over Rhyder's features "—I don't understand." It didn't make sense.

"I'm not surprised, you blind little fool," Rhyder growled. "The conversation between Pete and myself that you overheard this morning concerned having the annulment officially overturned. I knew Justin wanted you and he wouldn't be happy to find that you'd come back to me. As for the telephone call to my father, he knew about us and that I'd met you again and discovered I wanted you for my wife. The news I was referring to had nothing to do with the property. It was to tell him we'd been reconciled."

Her dark head pivoted stiffly from side to side in disbelief. "No," she protested, but he sounded so convincing.

"And a few moments ago with Justin," he continued without acknowledging her protest, "I did say that my decision about the property would depend on you. If you didn't come back to me, I wasn't buying the land. Because if I couldn't have you, I didn't want to set foot in Maine again for business or any other reason."

Gina's fingers closed around the agreement, unconsciously crumbling it into a ball. She wanted desperately to believe what he was saying, but her heart was afraid it was yet another trick.

"Why did you want me back, Rhyder?" she breathed, searching the hard planes of his face.

"What other reason is left, Gina," he demanded bitterly, "except that I love you?"

"You never said so. You only said you wanted me."

"Because I love you," he repeated grimly. "It's probably always been because I love you."

Her heart gave a leap of joy, no longer afraid to believe him. The deep abiding love she felt blazed in her eyes, but Rhyder didn't seem to see it.

"Come on, Gina," Pete prodded softly. "Tell him you love him so I can break out the bottle of champagne!"

Rhyder's head jerked at the words, his gaze narrowing. A tremulous smile curved her lips, a wild song singing through her viens.

"Do you remember something you told Justin?" Her voice was barely above a whisper, trembling with emotion. "You said our relationship was an equal amount of anger and passion. It's true. Even when I hated you, I loved you, Rhyder."

The arrogance seemed to leave him along with the bitterness. His hand reached out to tentatively trace the line of her temple. Her dark lashes fluttered in response to the caress.

In the next instant his arms were around her and his mouth was hungrily possessing her lips. Gina returned the insatiable need with all the pent-up longing of her heart. Neither heard the explosive pop of the champagne cork or the hiss of bubbling liquid being poured into a trio of glasses.

Pete smiled, picked up one of the glasses and quietly left the room. The champagne would be flat when Gina and Rhyder finally drank their toast.